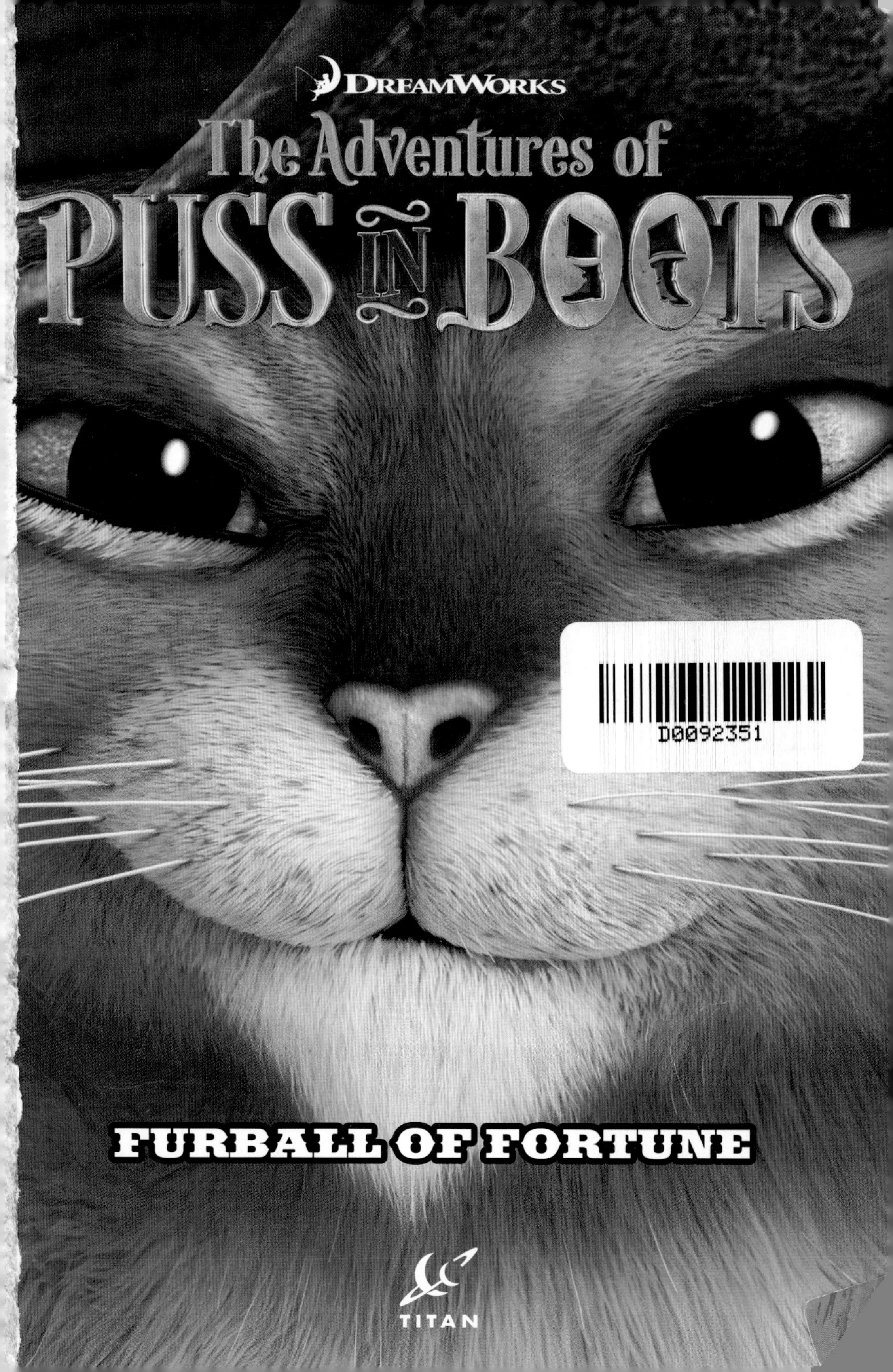
DreamWorks
The Adventures of
PUSS IN BOOTS
FURBALL OF FORTUNE
TITAN

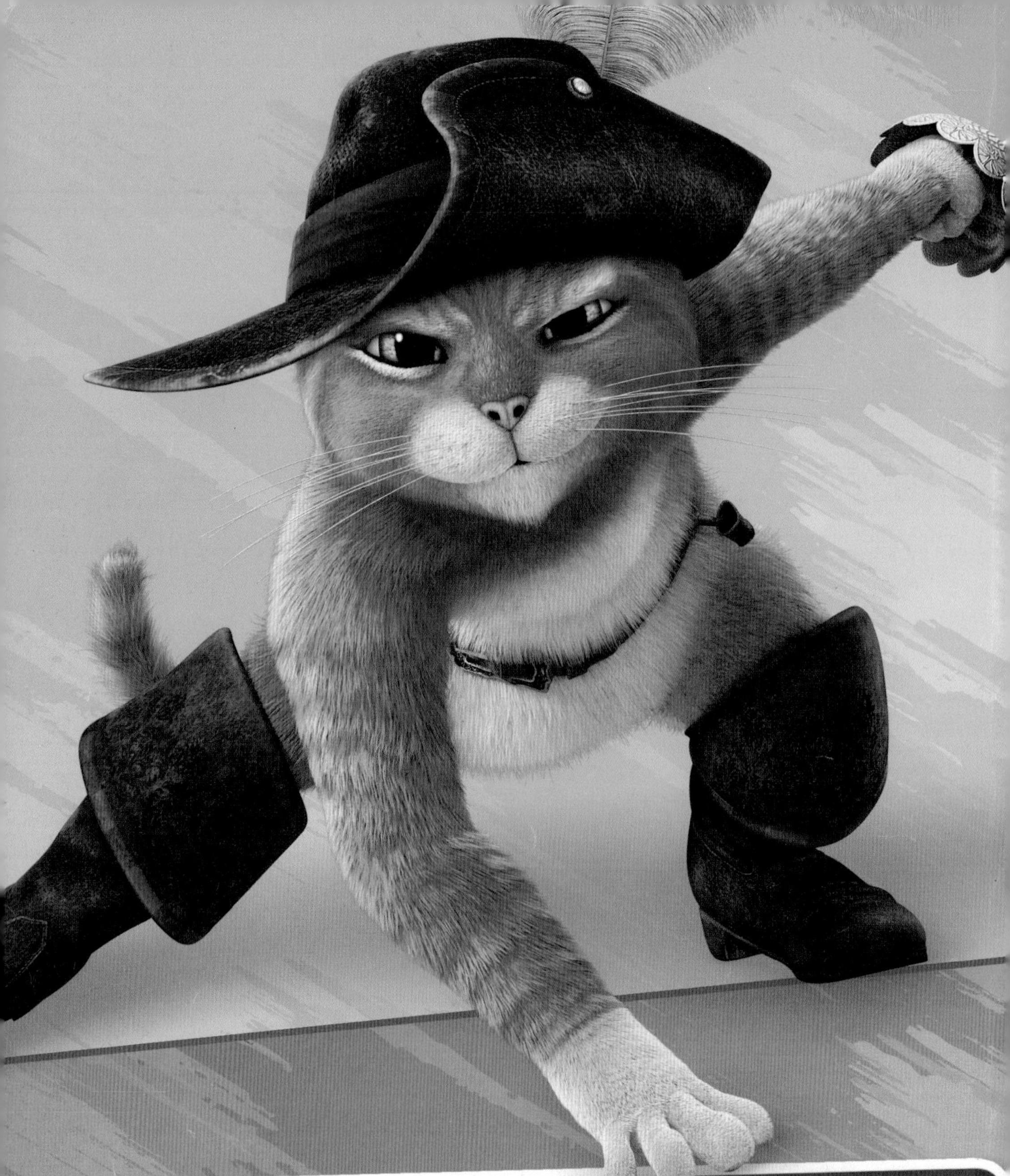

THIS BOOK IS BROUGHT TO YOU BY...

Editor Rona Simpson
Senior Editor Martin Eden
Production Manager Obi Onoura
Production Assistant Peter James
Production Supervisors Jackie Flook, Maria Pearson
Studio Manager Emma Smith
Circulation Manager Steve Tothill
Direct Sales & Marketing Manager Ricky Claydon
Publishing Manager Darryl Tothill
Publishing Director Chris Teather
Operations Director Leigh Baulch
Executive Director Vivian Cheung
Publisher Nick Landau

Puss in Boots Vol 1: Furball of Fortune
ISBN: 9781782853926

10 9 8 7 6 5 4 3 2 1

First printed in Lithuania in August 2016.

A CIP catalogue record for this title is available from the British Library.

TCN: 1535

Special thanks to Corinne Combs, Barbara Layman, and Lawrence Hamashima. Also, Andre Siregar at Glasshouse.

INSIDE... 2 AWESOME COMIC STRIPS

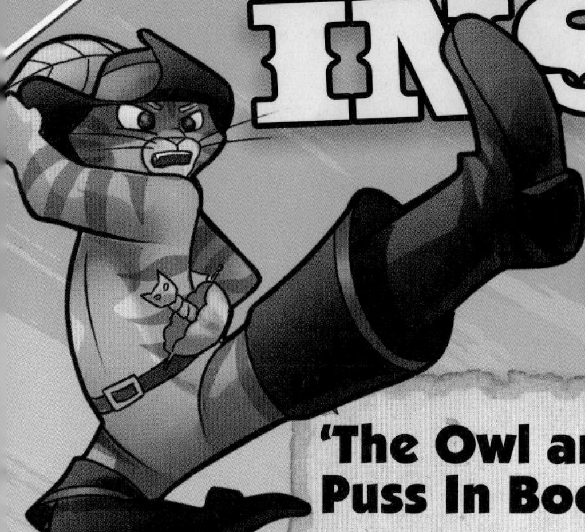

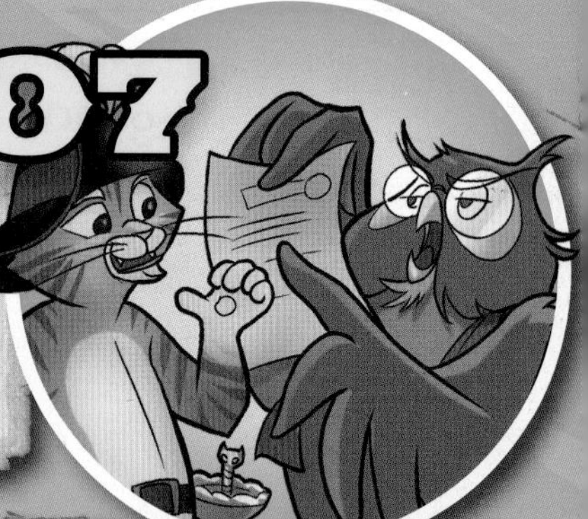

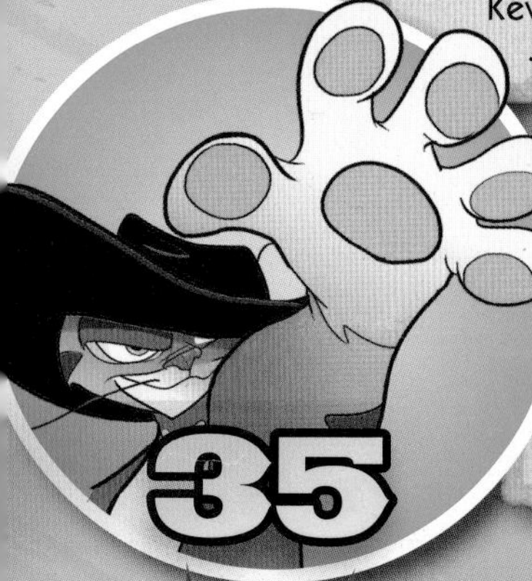

PLUS... 2 BONUS STORIES!!

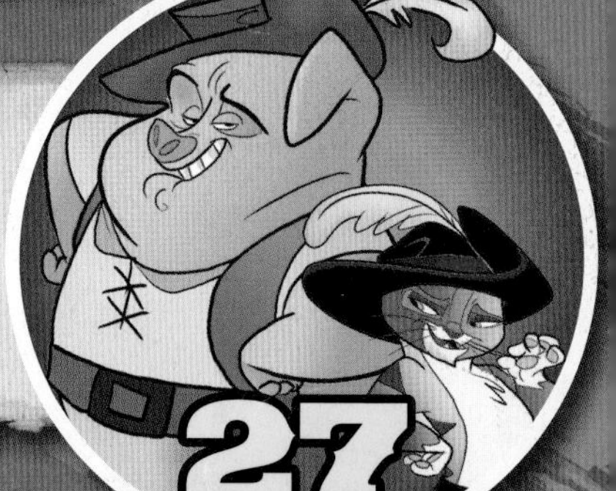

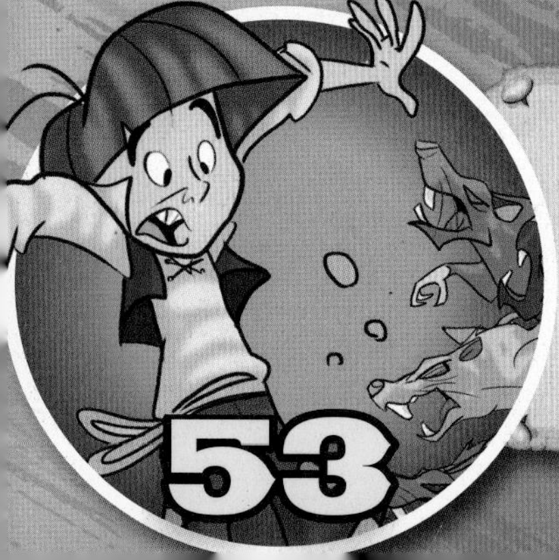

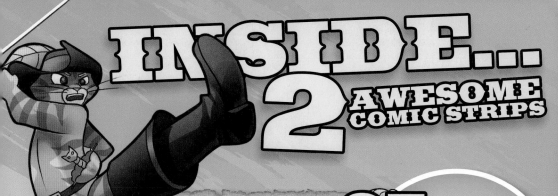

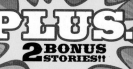

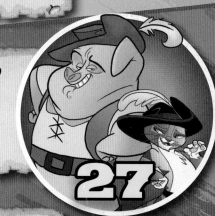

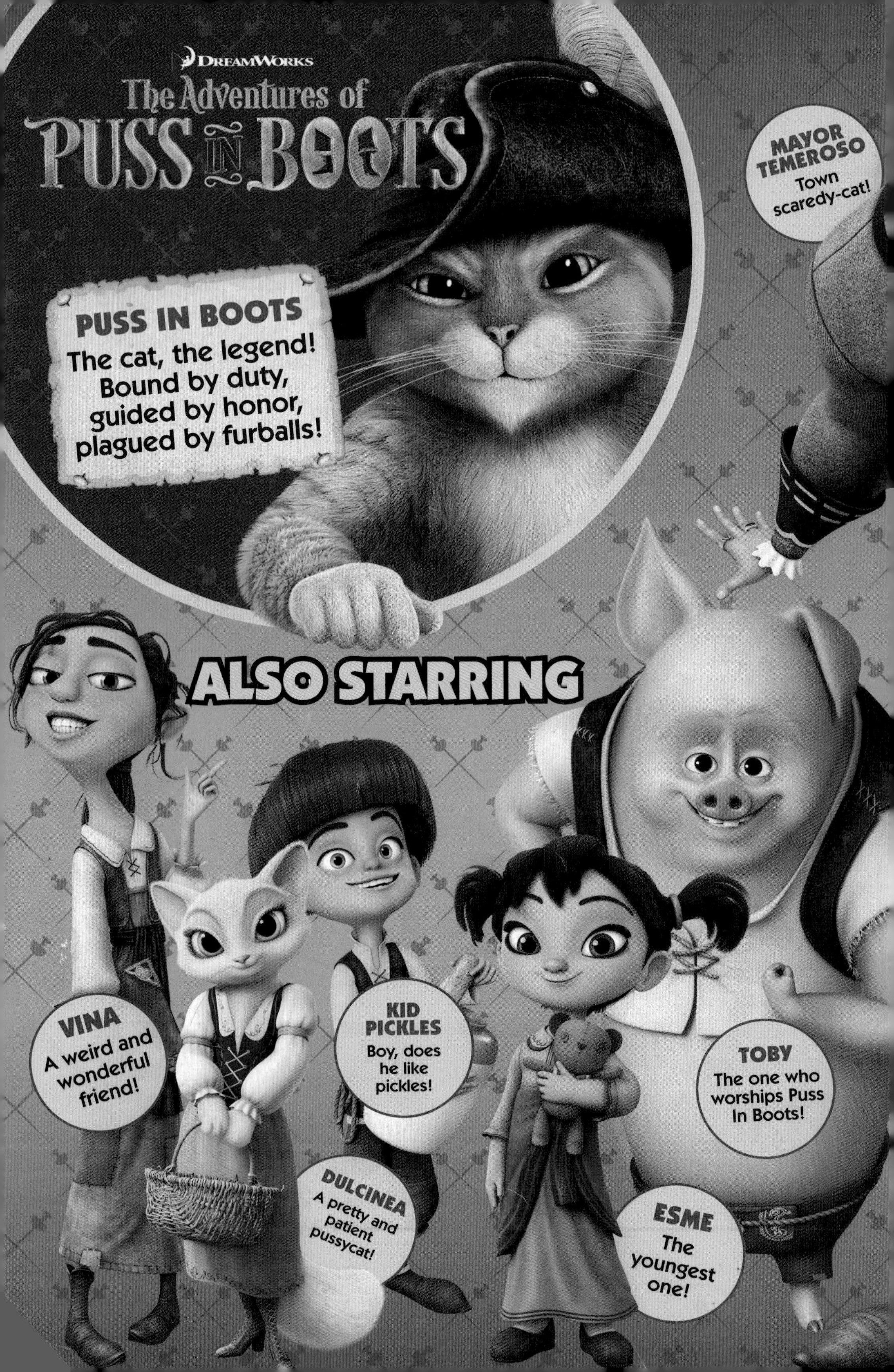
DreamWorks
The Adventures of
PUSS IN BOOTS
MAYOR TEMEROSO
Town scaredy-cat!
PUSS IN BOOTS
The cat, the legend! Bound by duty, guided by honor, plagued by furballs!
ALSO STARRING
VINA
A weird and wonderful friend!
KID PICKLES
Boy, does he like pickles!
TOBY
The one who worships Puss In Boots!
DULCINEA
A pretty and patient pussycat!
ESME
The youngest one!

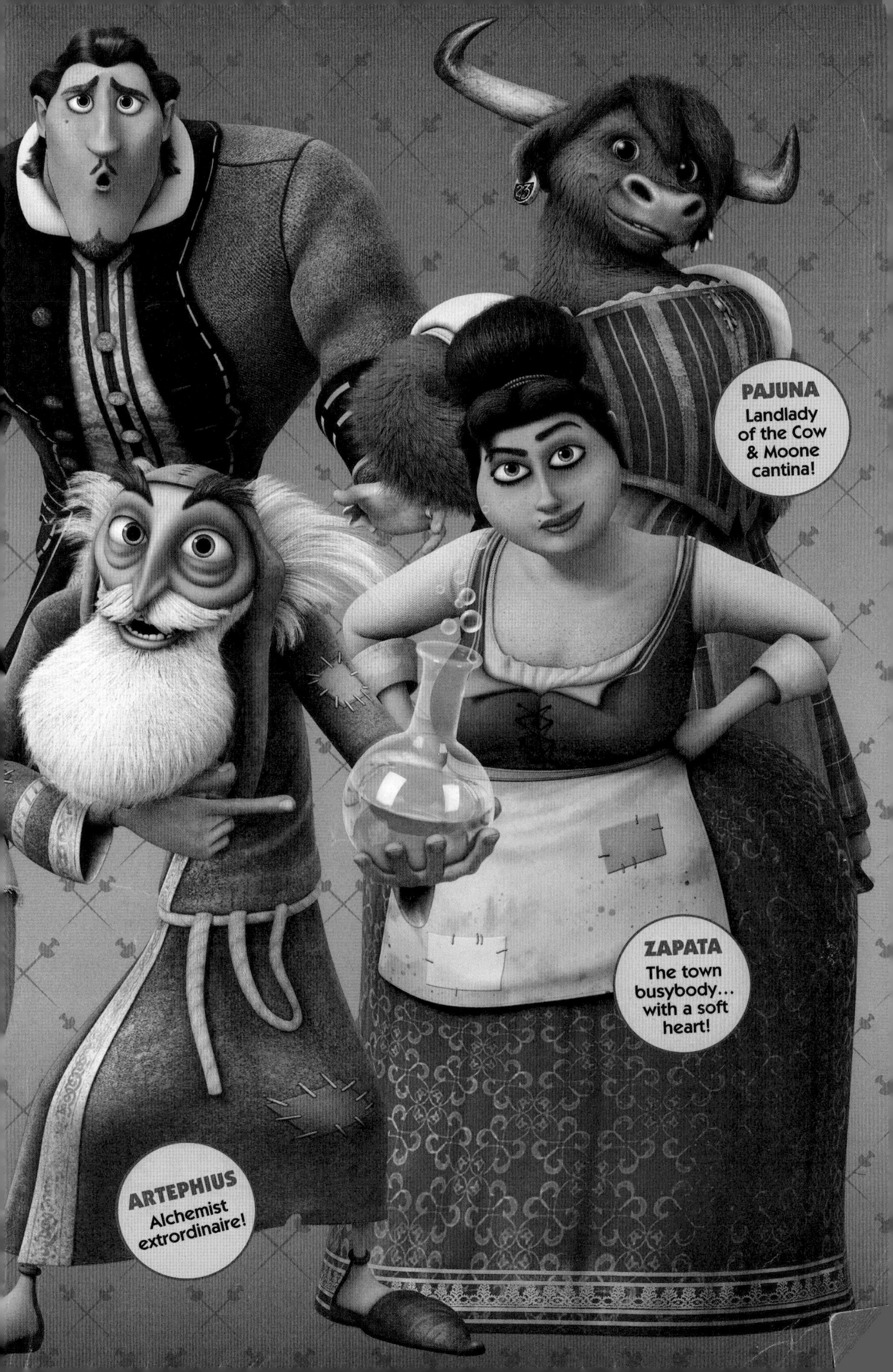
PAJUNA
Landlady of the Cow & Moone cantina!
ZAPATA
The town busybody... with a soft heart!
ARTEPHIUS
Alchemist extrordinaire!

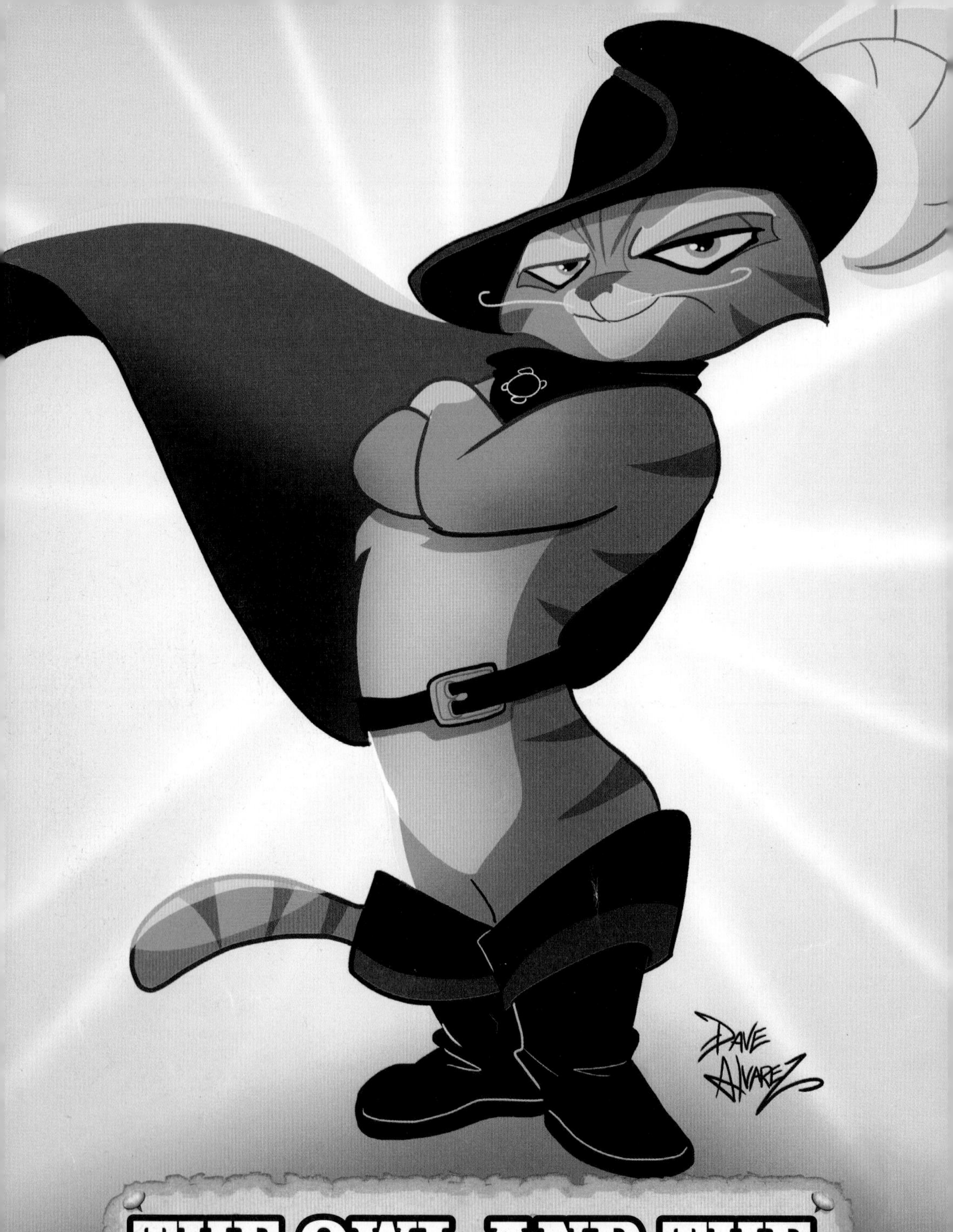
DAVE ALVAREZ

THE OWL AND THE PUSS IN BOOTS!

SCRIPT BY CHRIS COOPER • PENCILS BY EGLE BARTOLINI • INKS BY MARIA L SANAPO
COLORS BY VINCENTO SALVO AND KEVIN ENHART • LETTERING BY JIM CAMPBELL.

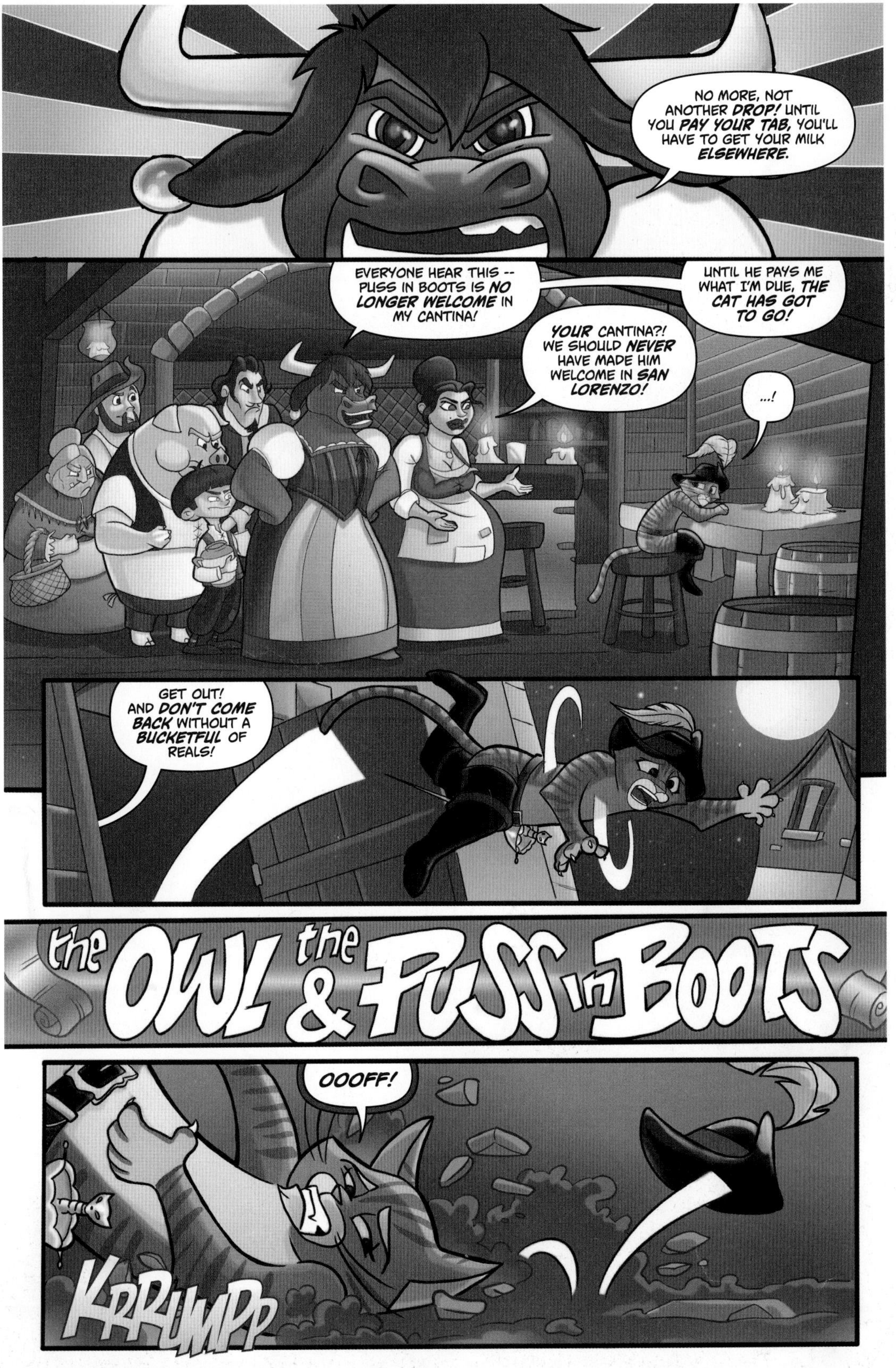
NO MORE, NOT ANOTHER DROP! UNTIL YOU PAY YOUR TAB, YOU'LL HAVE TO GET YOUR MILK ELSEWHERE.
EVERYONE HEAR THIS -- PUSS IN BOOTS IS NO LONGER WELCOME IN MY CANTINA!
UNTIL HE PAYS ME WHAT I'M DUE, THE CAT HAS GOT TO GO!
YOUR CANTINA?! WE SHOULD NEVER HAVE MADE HIM WELCOME IN SAN LORENZO!
...!
GET OUT! AND DON'T COME BACK WITHOUT A BUCKETFUL OF REALS!
the OWL & the PUSS in BOOTS
OOOFF!
KRRUMPP

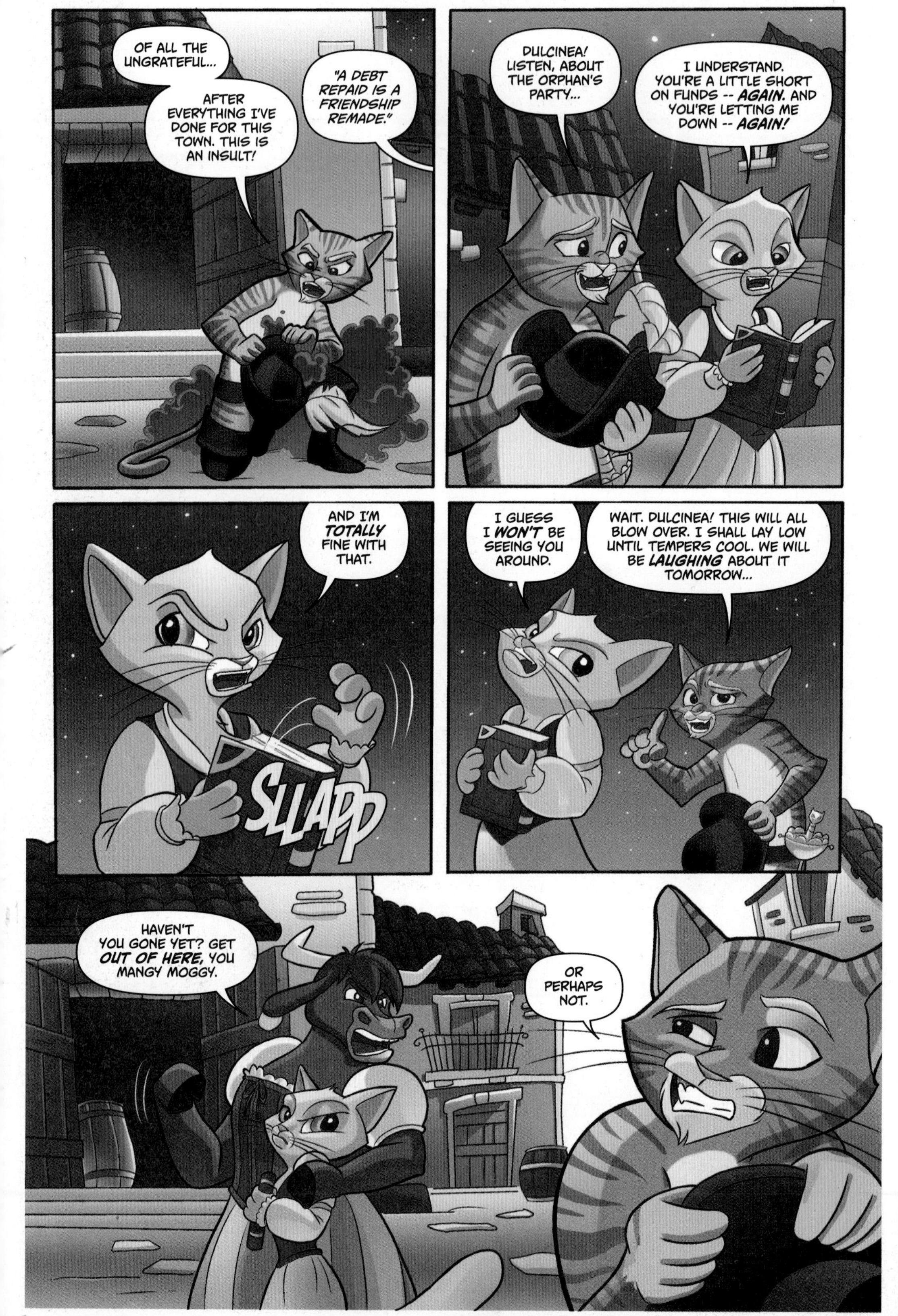
OF ALL THE UNGRATEFUL...
AFTER EVERYTHING I'VE DONE FOR THIS TOWN. THIS IS AN INSULT!
"A DEBT REPAID IS A FRIENDSHIP REMADE."
DULCINEA! LISTEN, ABOUT THE ORPHAN'S PARTY...
I UNDERSTAND. YOU'RE A LITTLE SHORT ON FUNDS -- AGAIN. AND YOU'RE LETTING ME DOWN -- AGAIN!
AND I'M TOTALLY FINE WITH THAT.
SLLAPP
I GUESS I WON'T BE SEEING YOU AROUND.
WAIT. DULCINEA! THIS WILL ALL BLOW OVER. I SHALL LAY LOW UNTIL TEMPERS COOL. WE WILL BE LAUGHING ABOUT IT TOMORROW...
HAVEN'T YOU GONE YET? GET OUT OF HERE, YOU MANGY MOGGY.
OR PERHAPS NOT.

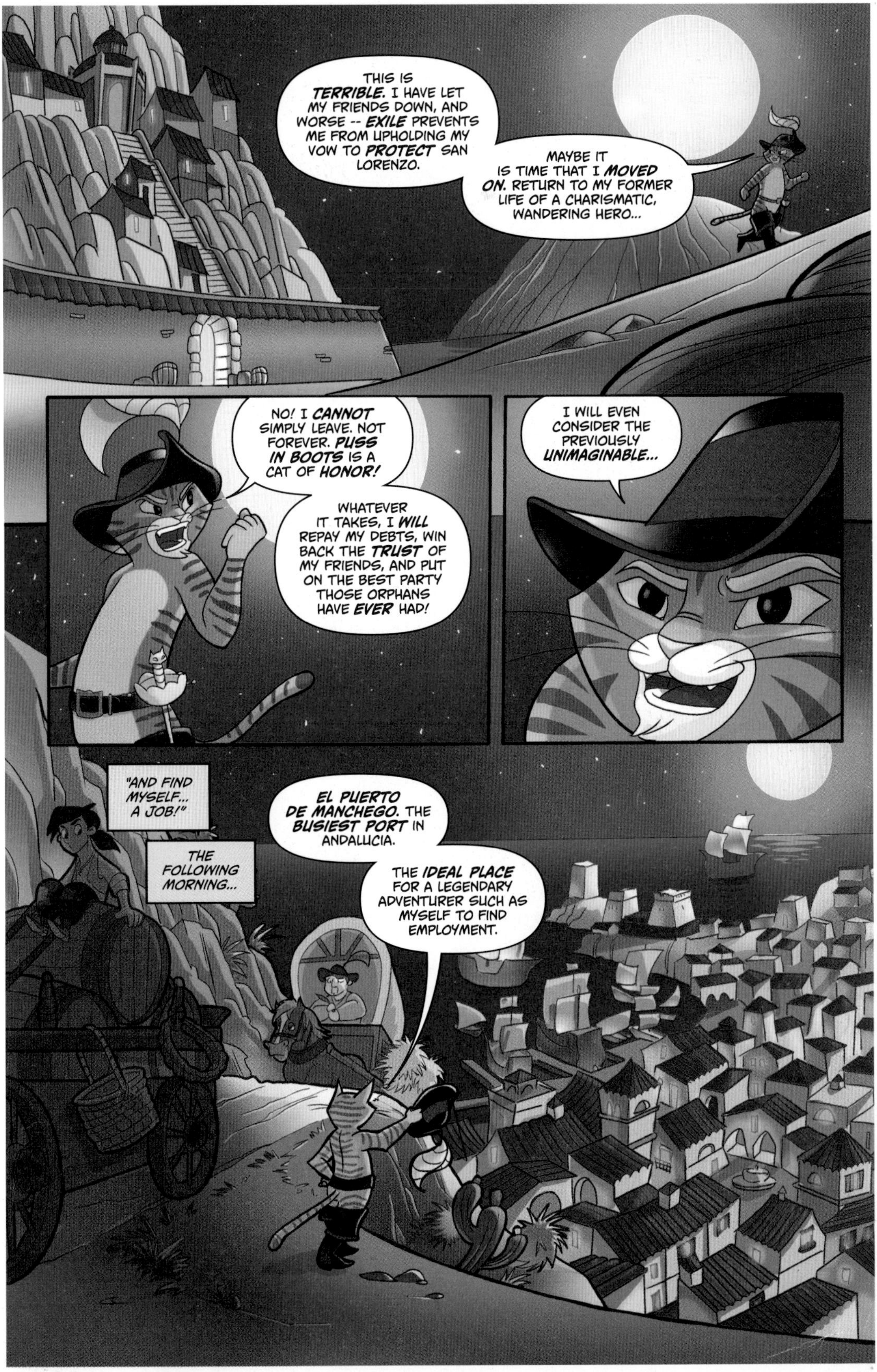
THIS IS TERRIBLE. I HAVE LET MY FRIENDS DOWN, AND WORSE -- EXILE PREVENTS ME FROM UPHOLDING MY VOW TO PROTECT SAN LORENZO.
MAYBE IT IS TIME THAT I MOVED ON. RETURN TO MY FORMER LIFE OF A CHARISMATIC, WANDERING HERO...
NO! I CANNOT SIMPLY LEAVE. NOT FOREVER. PUSS IN BOOTS IS A CAT OF HONOR!
WHATEVER IT TAKES, I WILL REPAY MY DEBTS, WIN BACK THE TRUST OF MY FRIENDS, AND PUT ON THE BEST PARTY THOSE ORPHANS HAVE EVER HAD!
I WILL EVEN CONSIDER THE PREVIOUSLY UNIMAGINABLE...
"AND FIND MYSELF... A JOB!"
THE FOLLOWING MORNING...
EL PUERTO DE MANCHEGO. THE BUSIEST PORT IN ANDALUCIA.
THE IDEAL PLACE FOR A LEGENDARY ADVENTURER SUCH AS MYSELF TO FIND EMPLOYMENT.

SITUATIONS VACANT

THE CLASSIFIED ADS. NOW LET ME SEE... "SITUATIONS VACANT"...

"PERFORMING MONKEY SEEKS ORGAN GRINDER."

A MANAGERIAL ROLE, YES, BUT HE IS ONLY PAYING PEANUTS.

Witch's familiar URGENTLY NEEDED Z'SIGHT A BONUS

PERFORMING MONKEY

Senior SALES REP. The MAGIC BEAN Co.

GIANT'S BAKERY SEEKS ENGLISHMAN

Pretty Polly Parrot AGENCY

TOP Pirates HIRING

DRAGON TRAINER

NORDIC ROOTS A MUST

MAKE$$$ WITH YOUR BUNIONS

DUNG COLLECTION

GIN

"DUNG COLLECTION OPERATIVE. SHOVEL SUPPLIED."

HMM. TEMPTING, BUT I HAVE AN ALLERGY.

AHA! THIS IS MORE LIKE IT!

MONEY, FOOD, AND ADVENTURE. IT HAS MY NAME WRITTEN ALL OVER IT!

NOW TO MAKE SURE THERE IS ONLY ONE PUSS FOR THE JOB.

OWL LOST

OWL seeks companion for HIGH ADVENTURE! competitive salary

Food and ACCOMMODATION INCLUDED

APPLY IN PERSON PIER 13, THE HARBOR

TERMS & CONDITION APPLY → SEE OVERLEAF

GIN

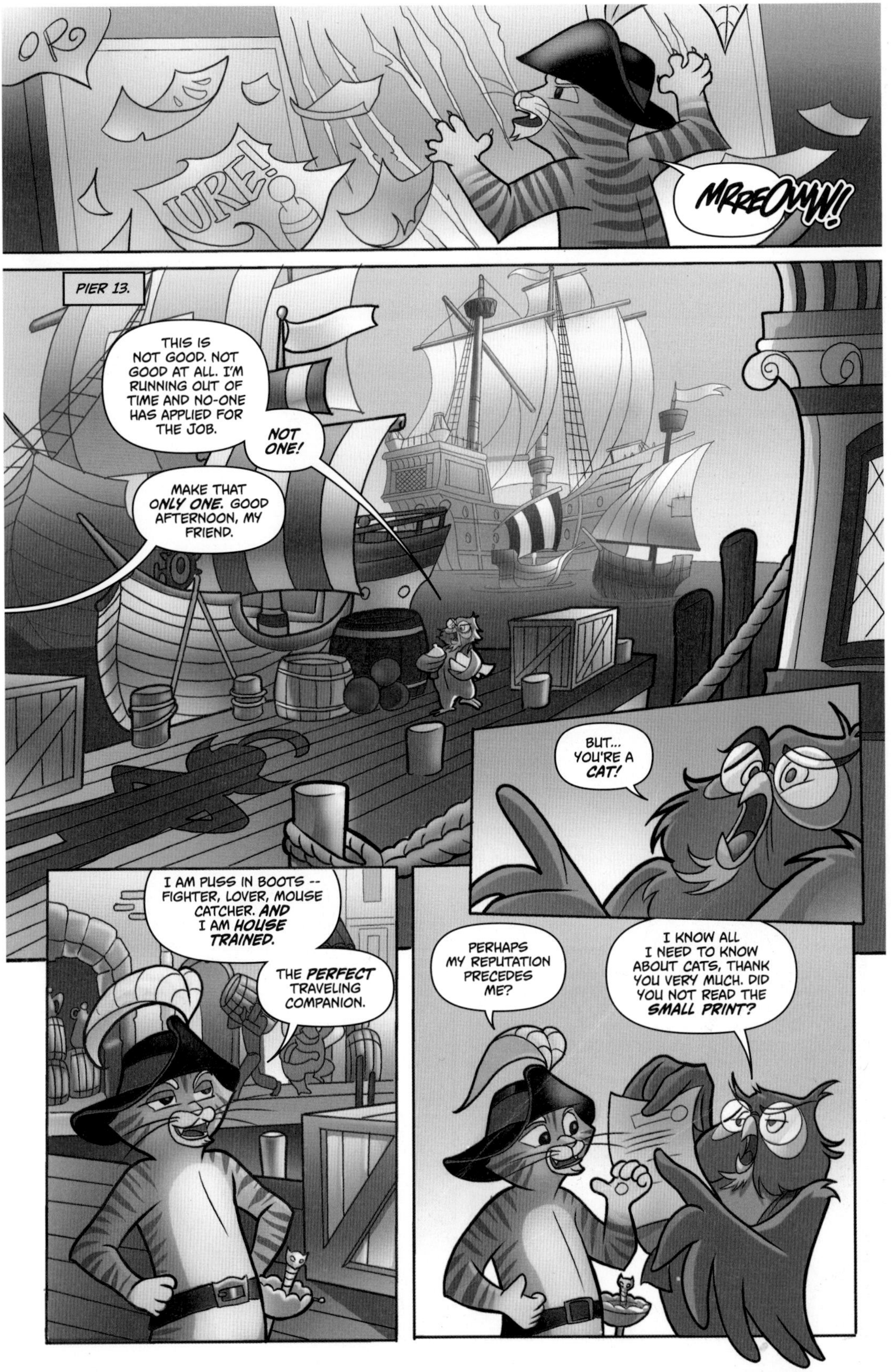
OR
URE!
MRREOWW!!
PIER 13.
THIS IS NOT GOOD. NOT GOOD AT ALL. I'M RUNNING OUT OF TIME AND NO-ONE HAS APPLIED FOR THE JOB.
NOT ONE!
MAKE THAT ONLY ONE. GOOD AFTERNOON, MY FRIEND.
BUT... YOU'RE A CAT!
I AM PUSS IN BOOTS -- FIGHTER, LOVER, MOUSE CATCHER. AND I AM HOUSE TRAINED.
THE PERFECT TRAVELING COMPANION.
PERHAPS MY REPUTATION PRECEDES ME?
I KNOW ALL I NEED TO KNOW ABOUT CATS, THANK YOU VERY MUCH. DID YOU NOT READ THE SMALL PRINT?

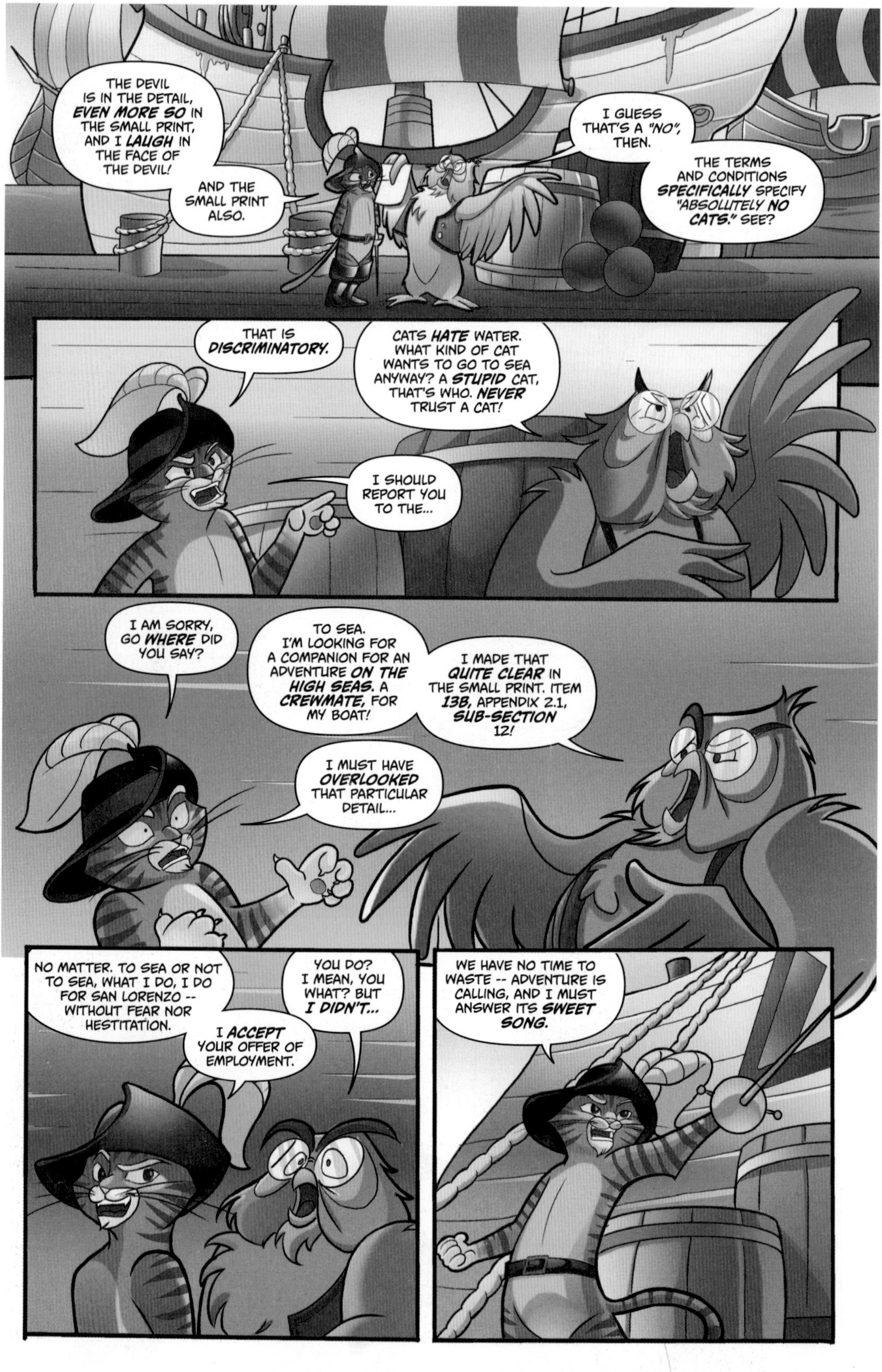
THE DEVIL IS IN THE DETAIL, EVEN MORE SO IN THE SMALL PRINT, AND I LAUGH IN THE FACE OF THE DEVIL!
AND THE SMALL PRINT ALSO.
I GUESS THAT'S A "NO", THEN.
THE TERMS AND CONDITIONS SPECIFICALLY SPECIFY "ABSOLUTELY NO CATS." SEE?
THAT IS DISCRIMINATORY.
CATS HATE WATER. WHAT KIND OF CAT WANTS TO GO TO SEA ANYWAY? A STUPID CAT, THAT'S WHO. NEVER TRUST A CAT!
I SHOULD REPORT YOU TO THE...
I AM SORRY, GO WHERE DID YOU SAY?
TO SEA. I'M LOOKING FOR A COMPANION FOR AN ADVENTURE ON THE HIGH SEAS. A CREWMATE, FOR MY BOAT!
I MADE THAT QUITE CLEAR IN THE SMALL PRINT. ITEM 13B, APPENDIX 2.1, SUB-SECTION 12!
I MUST HAVE OVERLOOKED THAT PARTICULAR DETAIL...
NO MATTER. TO SEA OR NOT TO SEA, WHAT I DO, I DO FOR SAN LORENZO -- WITHOUT FEAR NOR HESTITATION.
I ACCEPT YOUR OFFER OF EMPLOYMENT.
YOU DO? I MEAN, YOU WHAT? BUT I DIDN'T...
WE HAVE NO TIME TO WASTE -- ADVENTURE IS CALLING, AND I MUST ANSWER ITS SWEET SONG.

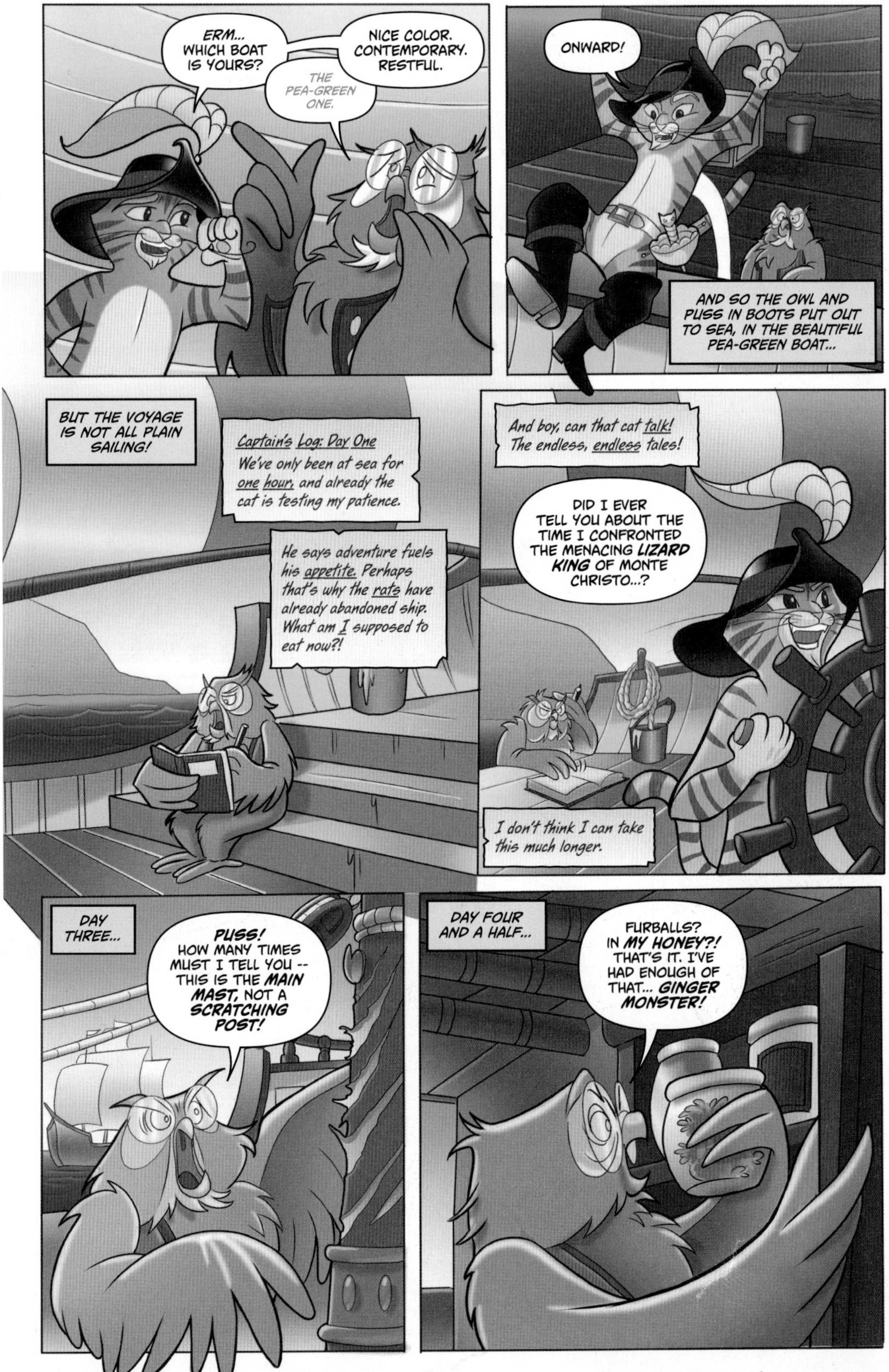
ERM... WHICH BOAT IS YOURS?
NICE COLOR. CONTEMPORARY. RESTFUL.
THE PEA-GREEN ONE.
ONWARD!
AND SO THE OWL AND PUSS IN BOOTS PUT OUT TO SEA, IN THE BEAUTIFUL PEA-GREEN BOAT...
BUT THE VOYAGE IS NOT ALL PLAIN SAILING!
Captain's Log: Day One
We've only been at sea for one hour, and already the cat is testing my patience.
He says adventure fuels his appetite. Perhaps that's why the rats have already abandoned ship. What am I supposed to eat now?!
And boy, can that cat talk! The endless, endless tales!
DID I EVER TELL YOU ABOUT THE TIME I CONFRONTED THE MENACING LIZARD KING OF MONTE CHRISTO...?
I don't think I can take this much longer.
DAY THREE...
PUSS! HOW MANY TIMES MUST I TELL YOU -- THIS IS THE MAIN MAST, NOT A SCRATCHING POST!
DAY FOUR AND A HALF...
FURBALLS? IN MY HONEY?! THAT'S IT. I'VE HAD ENOUGH OF THAT... GINGER MONSTER!

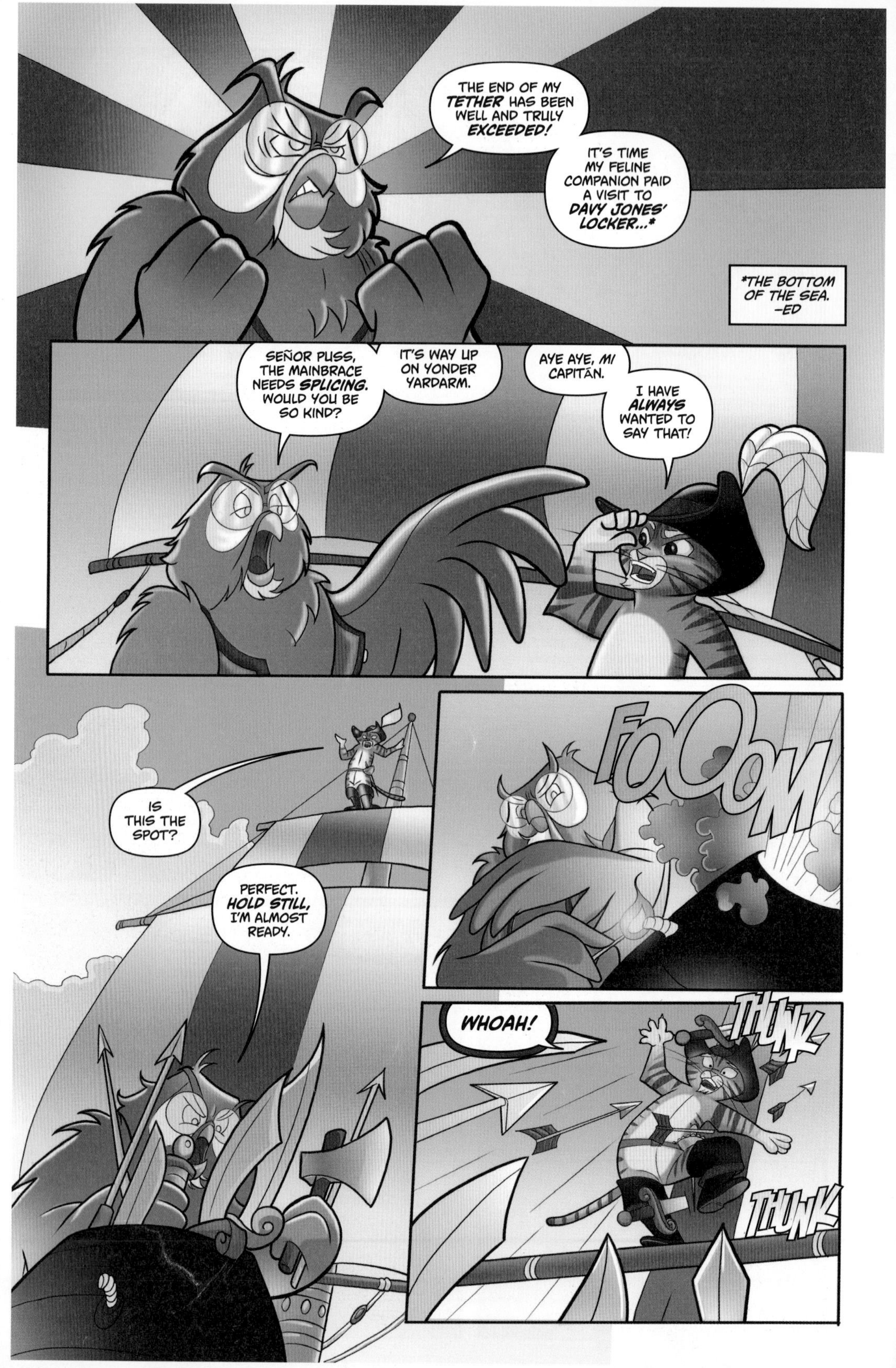
THE END OF MY TETHER HAS BEEN WELL AND TRULY EXCEEDED!
IT'S TIME MY FELINE COMPANION PAID A VISIT TO DAVY JONES' LOCKER...*
*THE BOTTOM OF THE SEA. -ED
SEÑOR PUSS, THE MAINBRACE NEEDS SPLICING. WOULD YOU BE SO KIND?
IT'S WAY UP ON YONDER YARDARM.
AYE AYE, MI CAPITÁN.
I HAVE ALWAYS WANTED TO SAY THAT!
IS THIS THE SPOT?
PERFECT. HOLD STILL, I'M ALMOST READY.
FOOOOM
WHOAH!
THUNK
THUNK

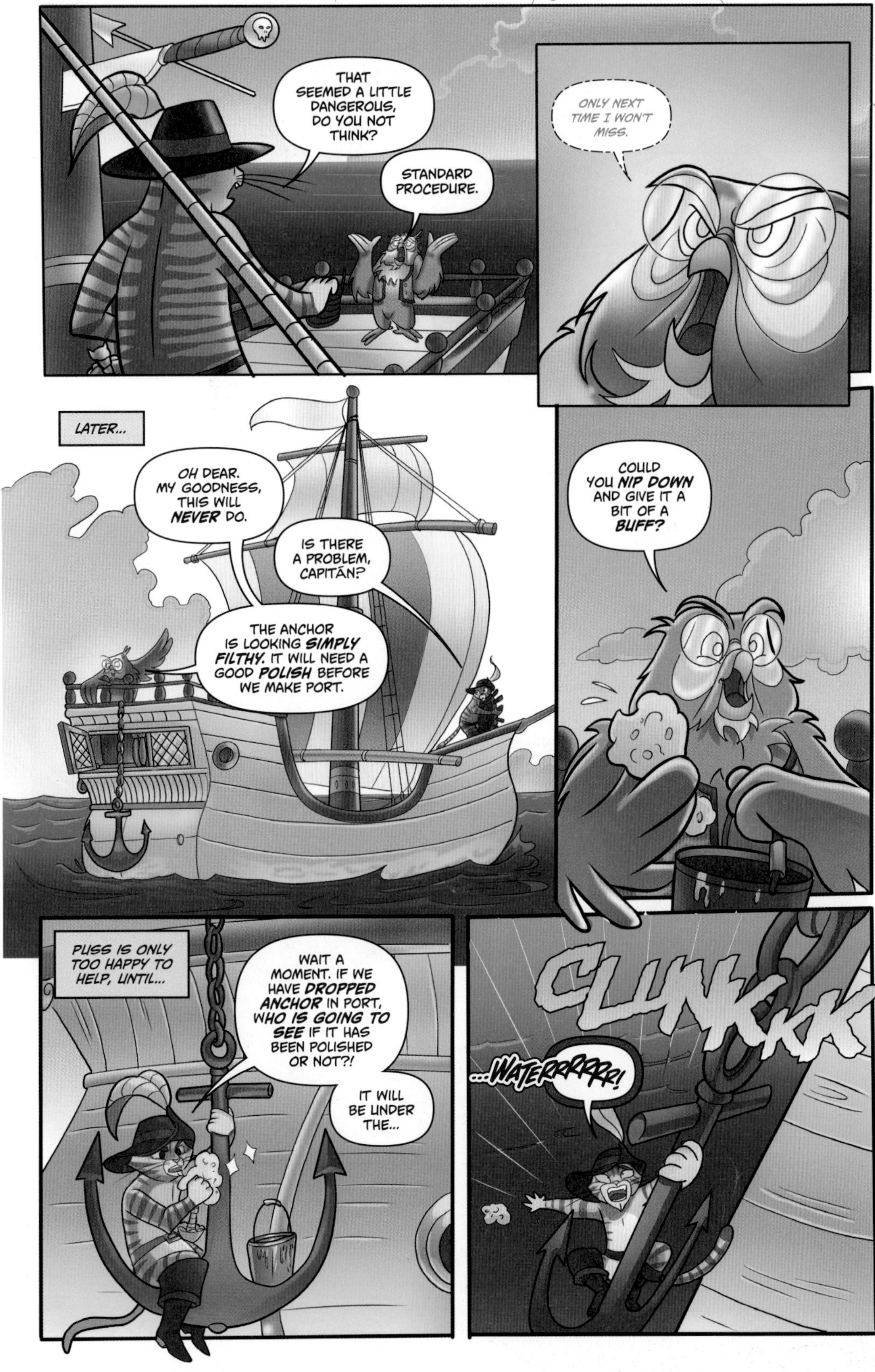
THAT SEEMED A LITTLE DANGEROUS, DO YOU NOT THINK?
STANDARD PROCEDURE.
ONLY NEXT TIME I WON'T MISS.
LATER...
OH DEAR. MY GOODNESS, THIS WILL NEVER DO.
IS THERE A PROBLEM, CAPITÁN?
THE ANCHOR IS LOOKING SIMPLY FILTHY. IT WILL NEED A GOOD POLISH BEFORE WE MAKE PORT.
COULD YOU NIP DOWN AND GIVE IT A BIT OF A BUFF?
PUSS IS ONLY TOO HAPPY TO HELP, UNTIL...
WAIT A MOMENT. IF WE HAVE DROPPED ANCHOR IN PORT, WHO IS GOING TO SEE IF IT HAS BEEN POLISHED OR NOT?!
IT WILL BE UNDER THE...
CLUNKKK
...WATERRRRRR!

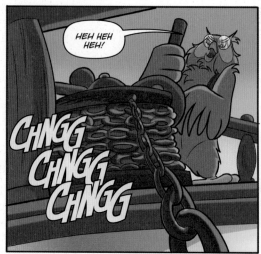

HEH HEH HEH!

CHNGG CHNGG CHNGG

SPLLSSHH

WOO HOO! NO MORE TALL TALES.

NO MORE HONEY-SOAKED FURBALLS.

NO MORE PUSS! HA HAH!

BUT...

NNGGG! I AM BEGINNING TO SUSPECT...

...MI CAPITÁN IS MORE OF A *DOG* PERSON.

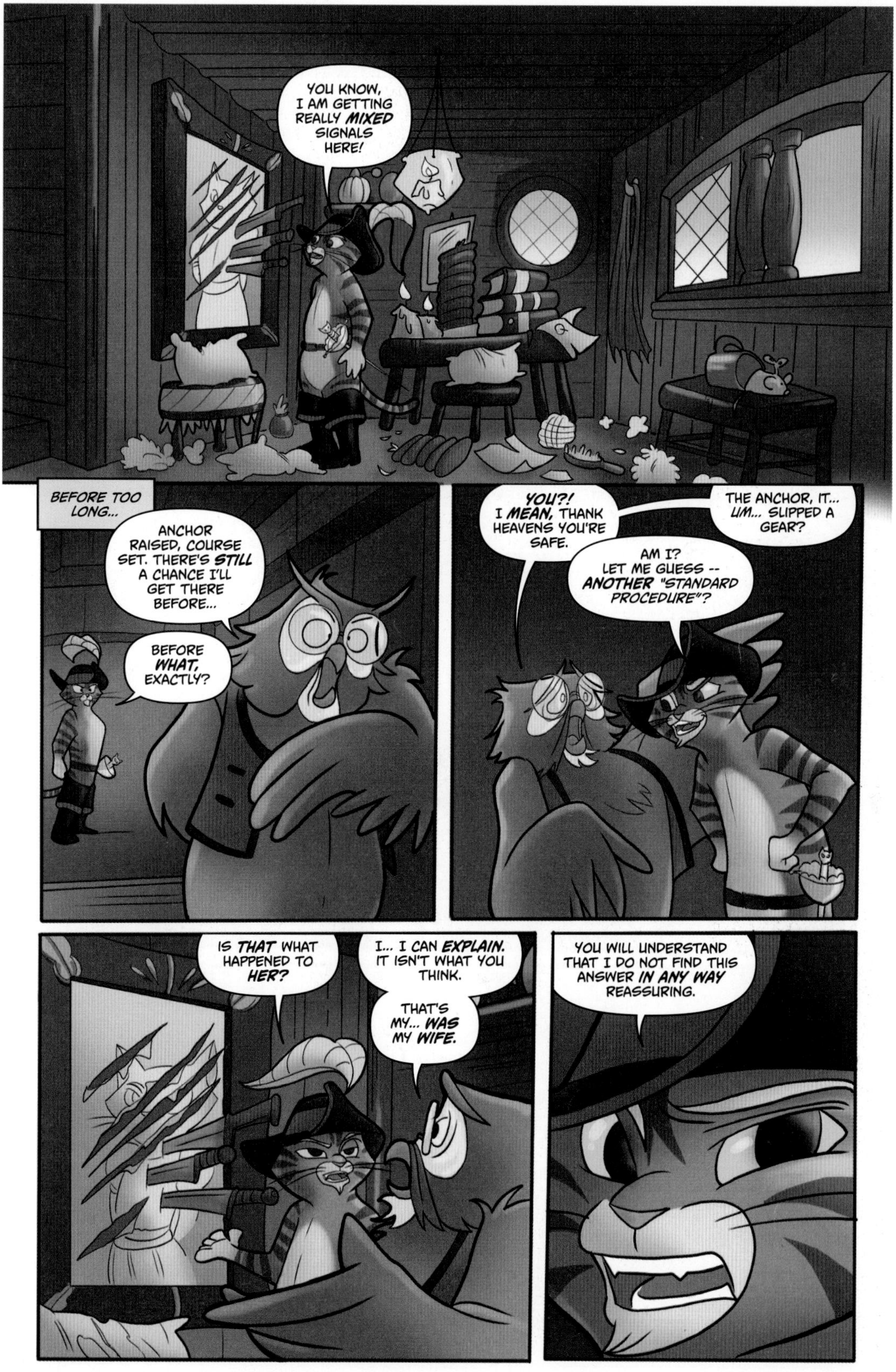
YOU KNOW, I AM GETTING REALLY MIXED SIGNALS HERE!
BEFORE TOO LONG...
ANCHOR RAISED, COURSE SET. THERE'S STILL A CHANCE I'LL GET THERE BEFORE...
BEFORE WHAT, EXACTLY?
YOU?! I MEAN, THANK HEAVENS YOU'RE SAFE.
THE ANCHOR, IT... UM... SLIPPED A GEAR?
AM I? LET ME GUESS -- ANOTHER "STANDARD PROCEDURE"?
IS THAT WHAT HAPPENED TO HER?
I... I CAN EXPLAIN. IT ISN'T WHAT YOU THINK.
THAT'S MY... WAS MY WIFE.
YOU WILL UNDERSTAND THAT I DO NOT FIND THIS ANSWER IN ANY WAY REASSURING.

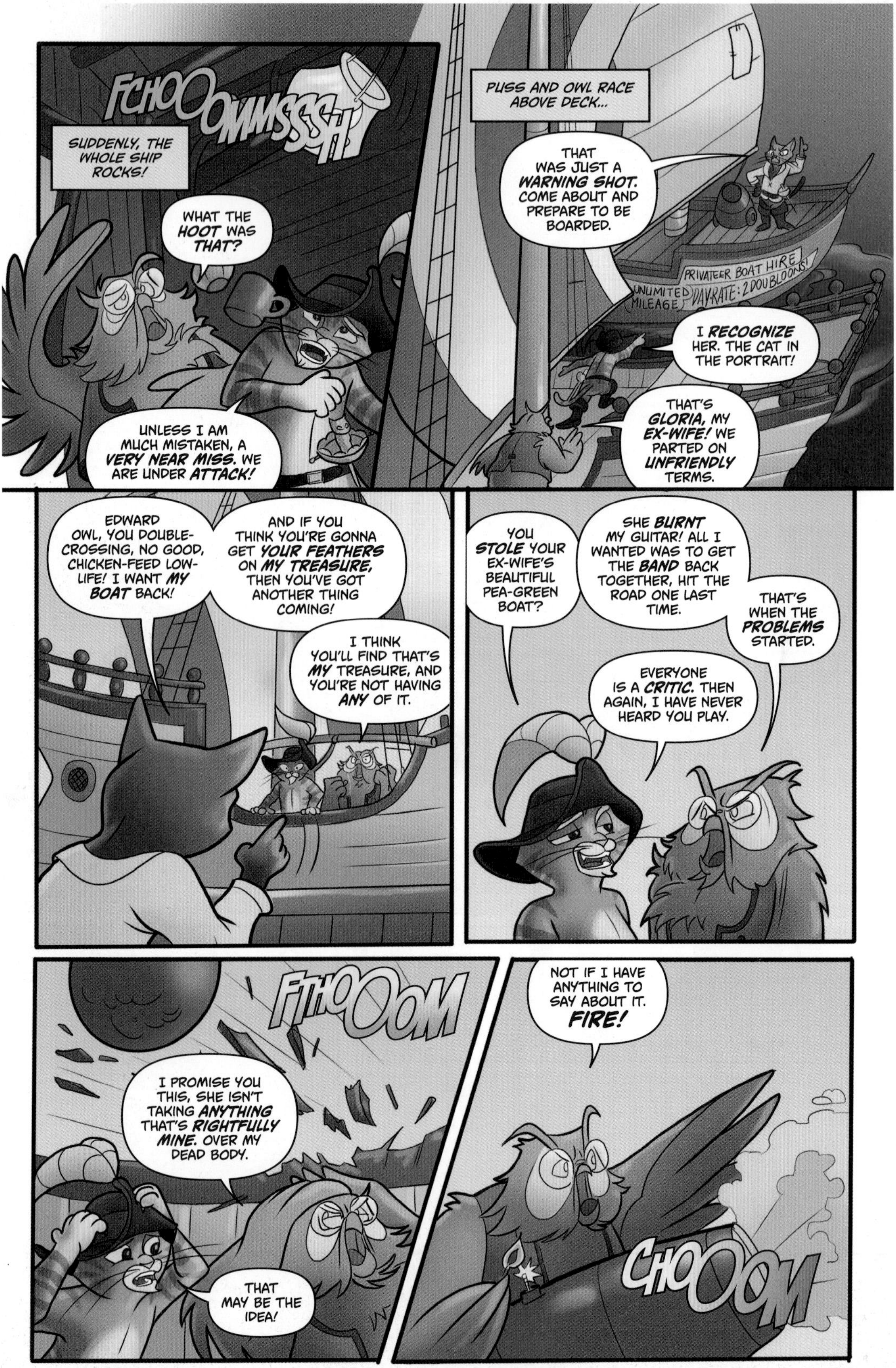
FCHOOOMMSSSSH
SUDDENLY, THE WHOLE SHIP ROCKS!
WHAT THE HOOT WAS THAT?
UNLESS I AM MUCH MISTAKEN, A VERY NEAR MISS. WE ARE UNDER ATTACK!
PUSS AND OWL RACE ABOVE DECK...
THAT WAS JUST A WARNING SHOT. COME ABOUT AND PREPARE TO BE BOARDED.
PRIVATEER BOAT HIRE
UNLIMITED MILEAGE
DAY RATE: 2 DOUBLOONS!
I RECOGNIZE HER. THE CAT IN THE PORTRAIT!
THAT'S GLORIA, MY EX-WIFE! WE PARTED ON UNFRIENDLY TERMS.
EDWARD OWL, YOU DOUBLE-CROSSING, NO GOOD, CHICKEN-FEED LOW-LIFE! I WANT MY BOAT BACK!
AND IF YOU THINK YOU'RE GONNA GET YOUR FEATHERS ON MY TREASURE, THEN YOU'VE GOT ANOTHER THING COMING!
I THINK YOU'LL FIND THAT'S MY TREASURE, AND YOU'RE NOT HAVING ANY OF IT.
YOU STOLE YOUR EX-WIFE'S BEAUTIFUL PEA-GREEN BOAT?
SHE BURNT MY GUITAR! ALL I WANTED WAS TO GET THE BAND BACK TOGETHER, HIT THE ROAD ONE LAST TIME.
THAT'S WHEN THE PROBLEMS STARTED.
EVERYONE IS A CRITIC. THEN AGAIN, I HAVE NEVER HEARD YOU PLAY.
FTHOOOOM
I PROMISE YOU THIS, SHE ISN'T TAKING ANYTHING THAT'S RIGHTFULLY MINE. OVER MY DEAD BODY.
THAT MAY BE THE IDEA!
NOT IF I HAVE ANYTHING TO SAY ABOUT IT. FIRE!
CHOOOOM

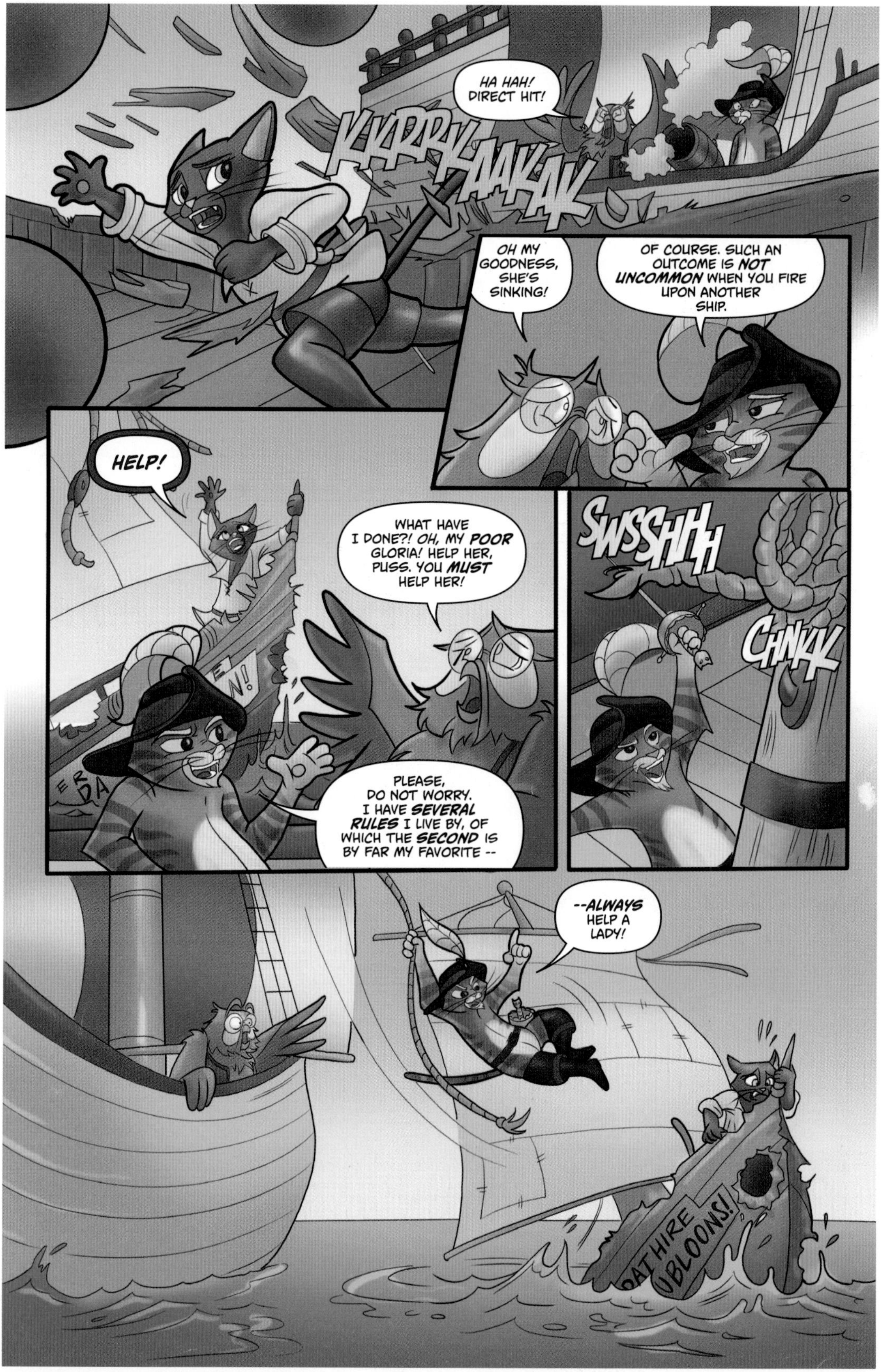
HA HAH! DIRECT HIT!
KKRRK KAAKAK
OH MY GOODNESS, SHE'S SINKING!
OF COURSE. SUCH AN OUTCOME IS NOT UNCOMMON WHEN YOU FIRE UPON ANOTHER SHIP.
HELP!
WHAT HAVE I DONE?! OH, MY POOR GLORIA! HELP HER, PUSS. YOU MUST HELP HER!
PLEASE, DO NOT WORRY. I HAVE SEVERAL RULES I LIVE BY, OF WHICH THE SECOND IS BY FAR MY FAVORITE --
SWSSHHH
CHNKK
--ALWAYS HELP A LADY!

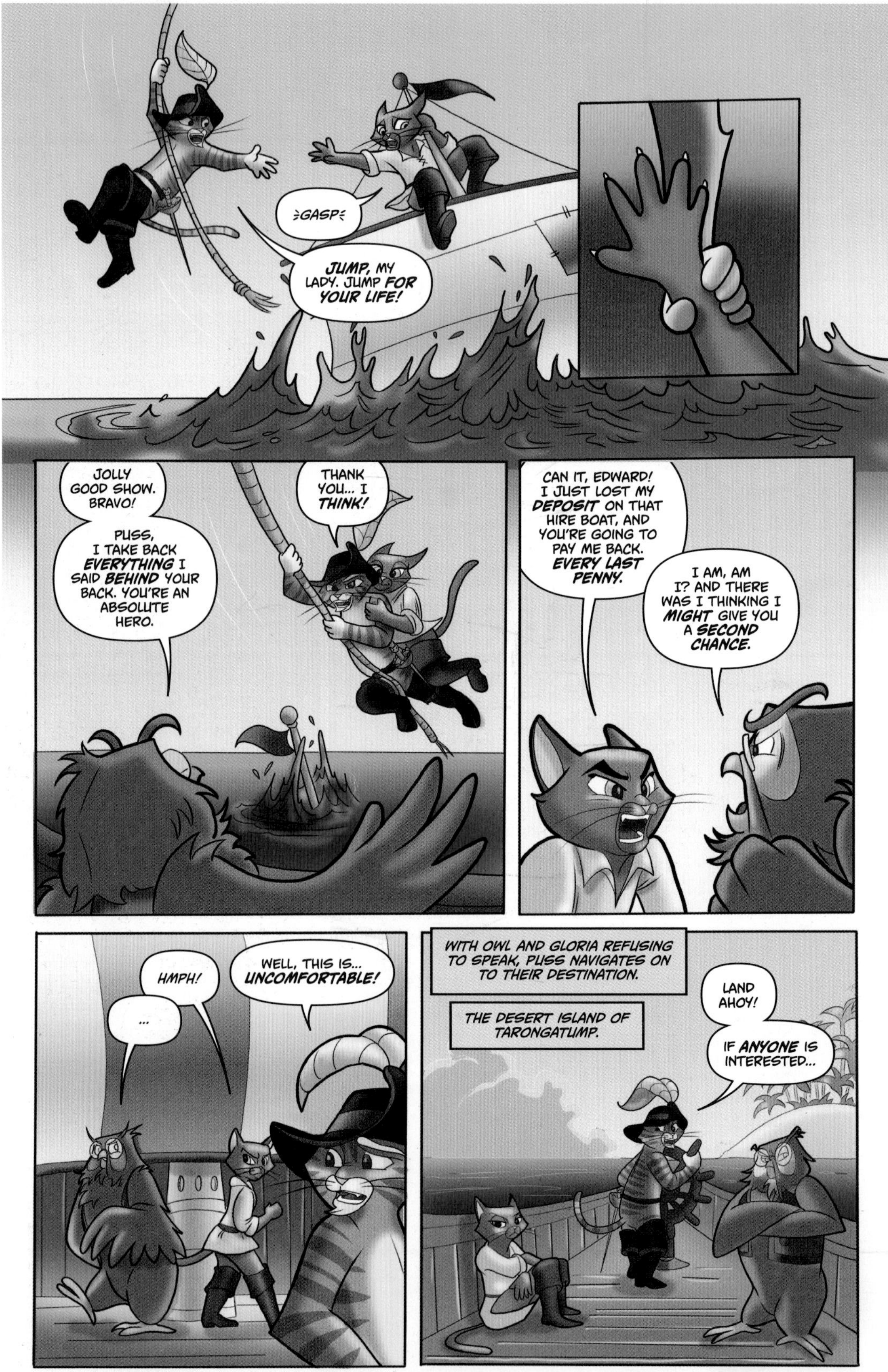

GASP
JUMP, MY LADY. JUMP FOR YOUR LIFE!
JOLLY GOOD SHOW. BRAVO!
PUSS, I TAKE BACK EVERYTHING I SAID BEHIND YOUR BACK. YOU'RE AN ABSOLUTE HERO.
THANK YOU... I THINK!
CAN IT, EDWARD! I JUST LOST MY DEPOSIT ON THAT HIRE BOAT, AND YOU'RE GOING TO PAY ME BACK. EVERY LAST PENNY.
I AM, AM I? AND THERE WAS I THINKING I MIGHT GIVE YOU A SECOND CHANCE.
HMPH!
...
WELL, THIS IS... UNCOMFORTABLE!
WITH OWL AND GLORIA REFUSING TO SPEAK, PUSS NAVIGATES ON TO THEIR DESTINATION.
THE DESERT ISLAND OF TARONGATUMP.
LAND AHOY!
IF ANYONE IS INTERESTED...

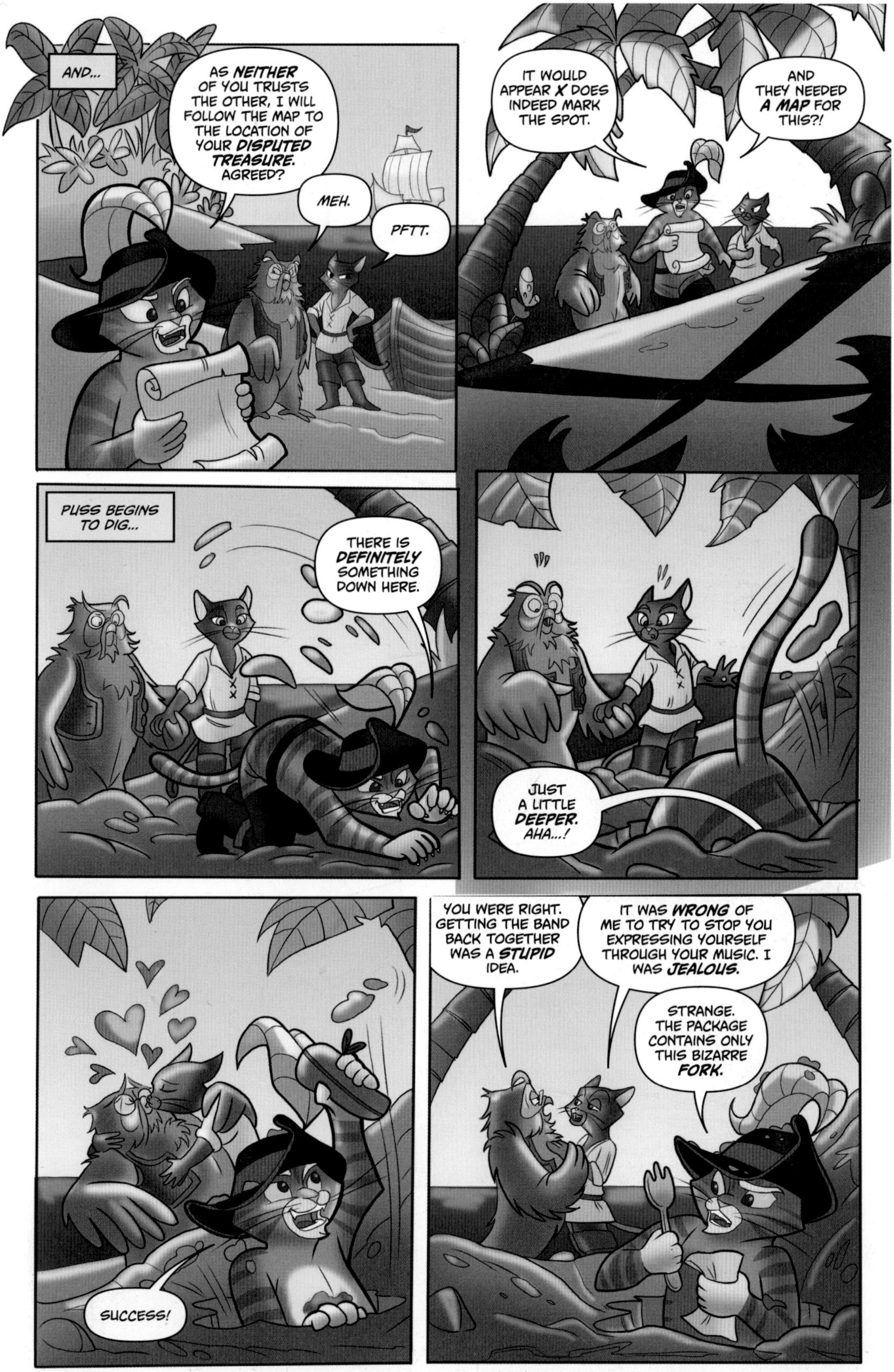
AND...
AS NEITHER OF YOU TRUSTS THE OTHER, I WILL FOLLOW THE MAP TO THE LOCATION OF YOUR DISPUTED TREASURE. AGREED?
MEH.
PFTT.
IT WOULD APPEAR X DOES INDEED MARK THE SPOT.
AND THEY NEEDED A MAP FOR THIS?!
PUSS BEGINS TO DIG...
THERE IS DEFINITELY SOMETHING DOWN HERE.
JUST A LITTLE DEEPER. AHA...!
SUCCESS!
YOU WERE RIGHT. GETTING THE BAND BACK TOGETHER WAS A STUPID IDEA.
IT WAS WRONG OF ME TO TRY TO STOP YOU EXPRESSING YOURSELF THROUGH YOUR MUSIC. I WAS JEALOUS.
STRANGE. THE PACKAGE CONTAINS ONLY THIS BIZARRE FORK.

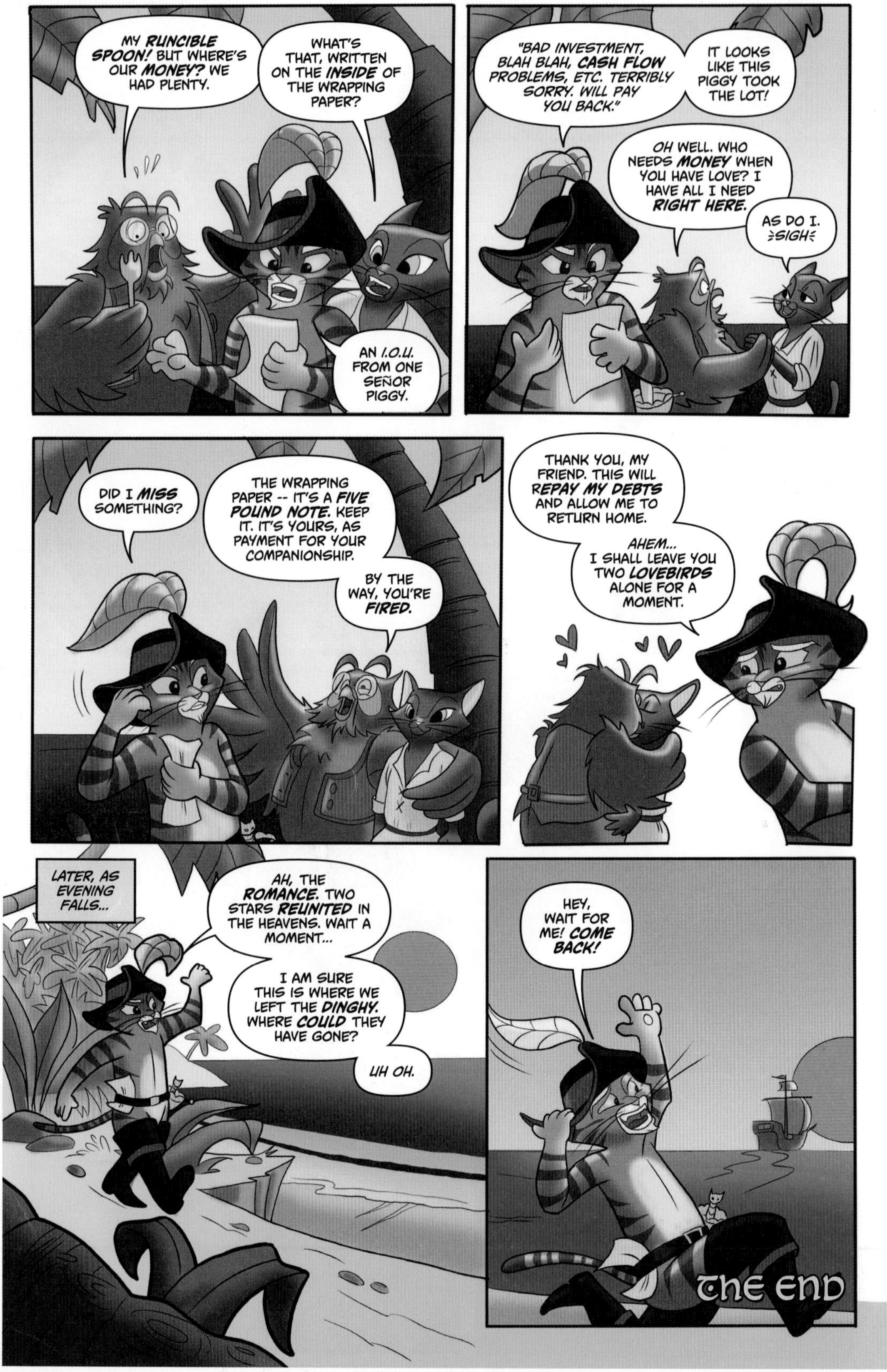

MY RUNCIBLE SPOON! BUT WHERE'S OUR MONEY? WE HAD PLENTY.
WHAT'S THAT, WRITTEN ON THE INSIDE OF THE WRAPPING PAPER?
AN I.O.U. FROM ONE SEÑOR PIGGY.
"BAD INVESTMENT, BLAH BLAH, CASH FLOW PROBLEMS, ETC. TERRIBLY SORRY. WILL PAY YOU BACK."
IT LOOKS LIKE THIS PIGGY TOOK THE LOT!
OH WELL. WHO NEEDS MONEY WHEN YOU HAVE LOVE? I HAVE ALL I NEED RIGHT HERE.
AS DO I. SIGH
DID I MISS SOMETHING?
THE WRAPPING PAPER -- IT'S A FIVE POUND NOTE. KEEP IT. IT'S YOURS, AS PAYMENT FOR YOUR COMPANIONSHIP.
BY THE WAY, YOU'RE FIRED.
THANK YOU, MY FRIEND. THIS WILL REPAY MY DEBTS AND ALLOW ME TO RETURN HOME.
AHEM... I SHALL LEAVE YOU TWO LOVEBIRDS ALONE FOR A MOMENT.
LATER, AS EVENING FALLS...
AH, THE ROMANCE. TWO STARS REUNITED IN THE HEAVENS. WAIT A MOMENT...
I AM SURE THIS IS WHERE WE LEFT THE DINGHY. WHERE COULD THEY HAVE GONE?
UH OH.
HEY, WAIT FOR ME! COME BACK!
THE END

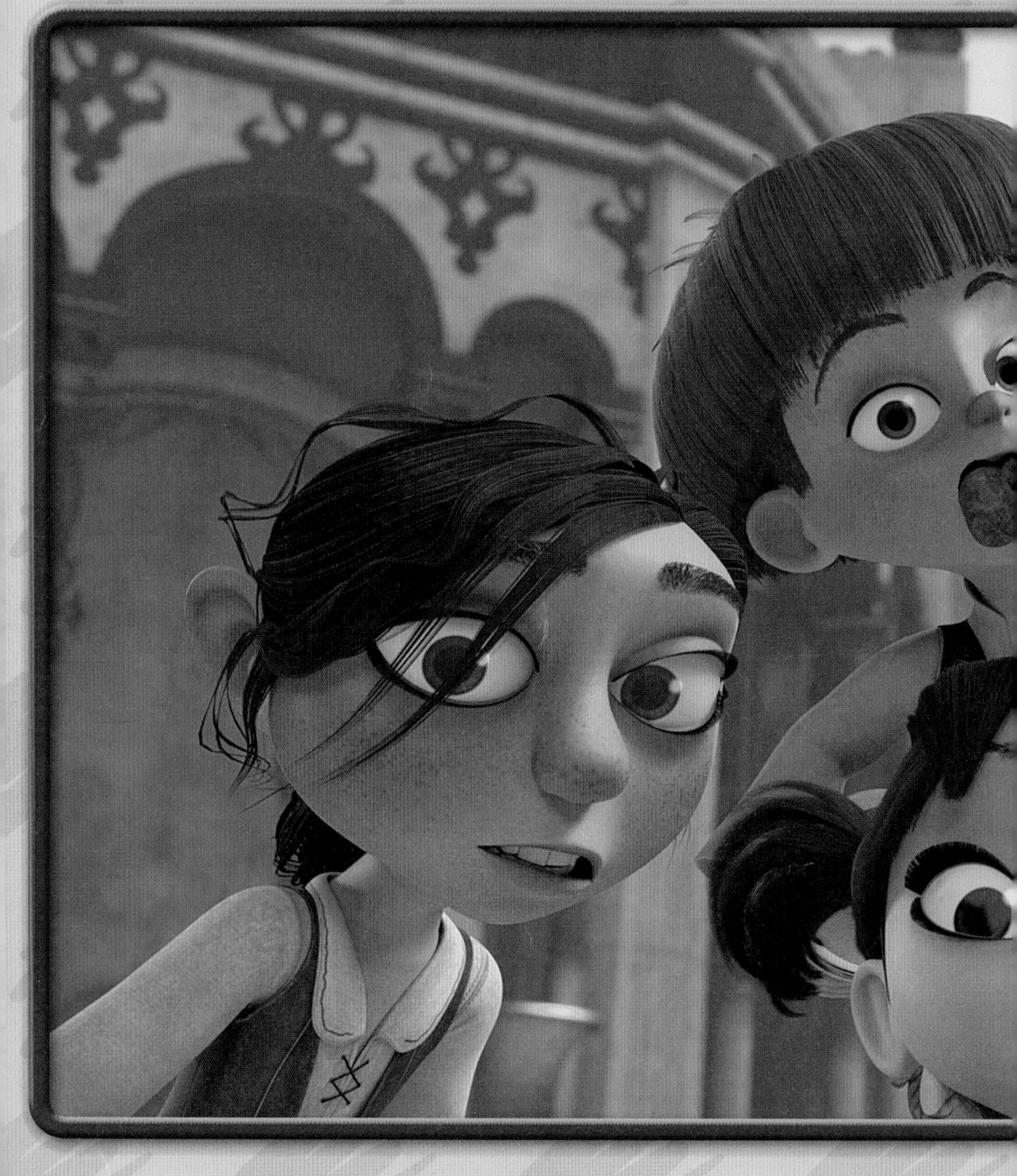

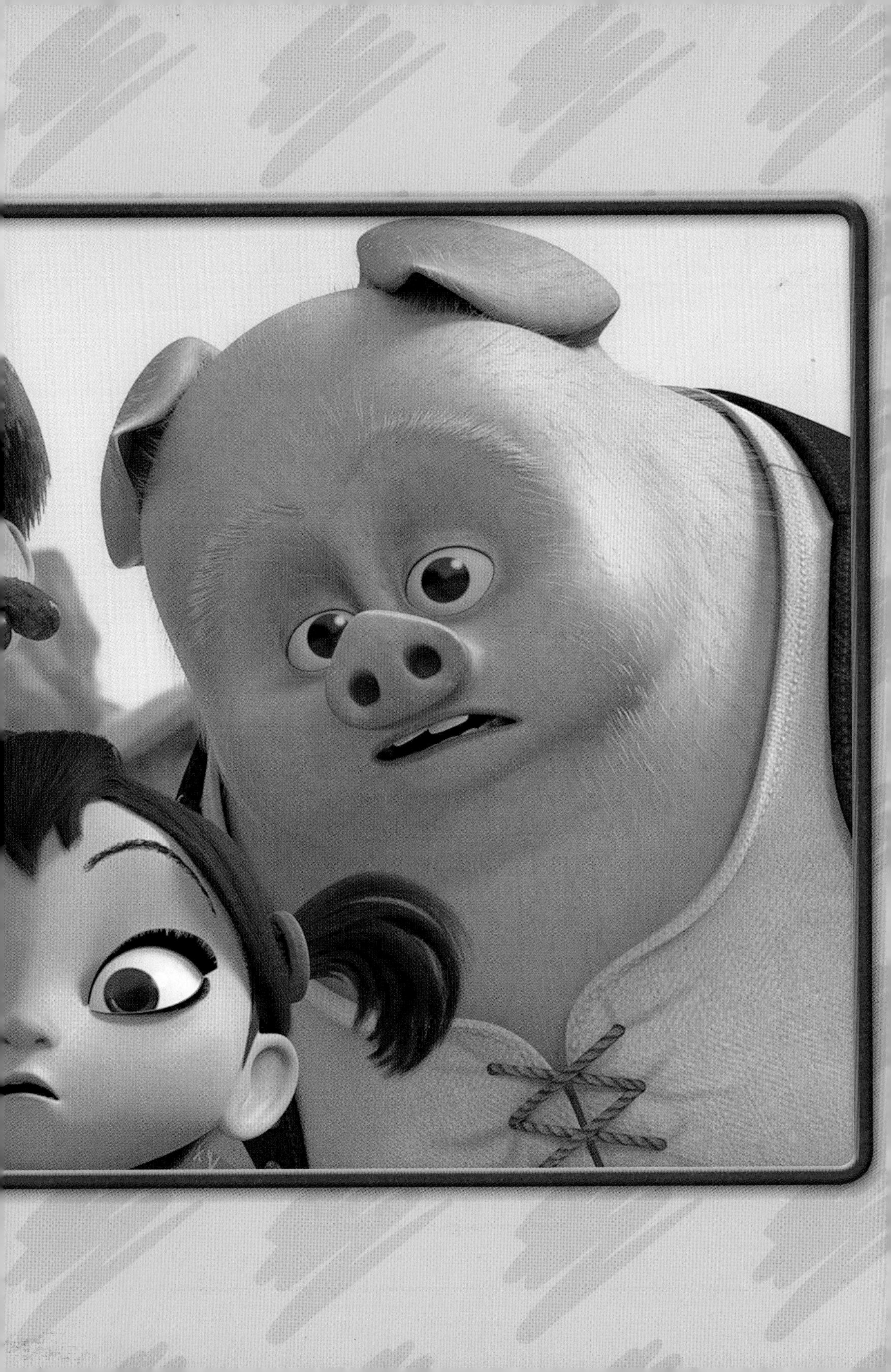

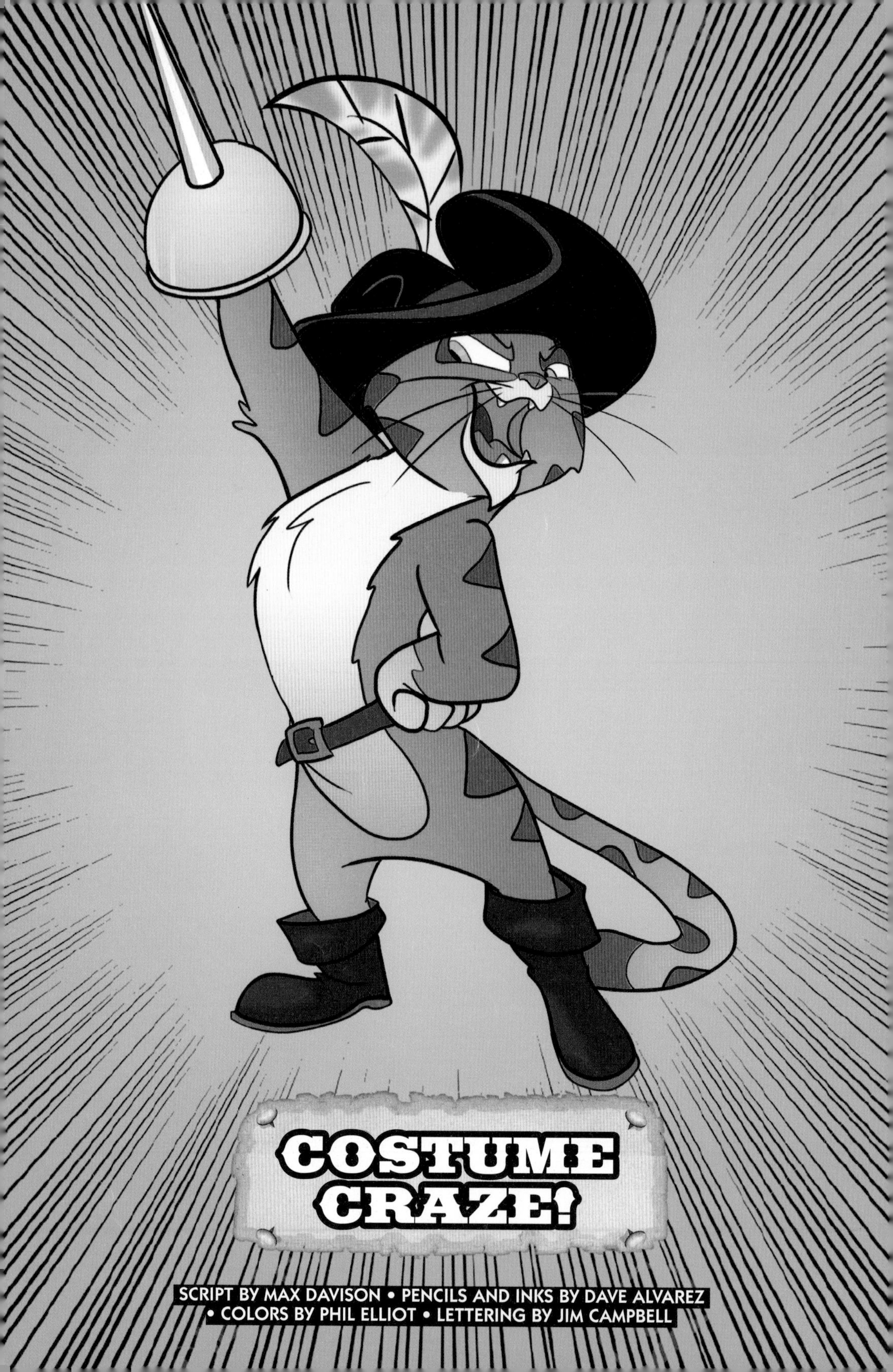
COSTUME
CRAZE!
SCRIPT BY MAX DAVISON • PENCILS AND INKS BY DAVE ALVAREZ
• COLORS BY PHIL ELLIOT • LETTERING BY JIM CAMPBELL

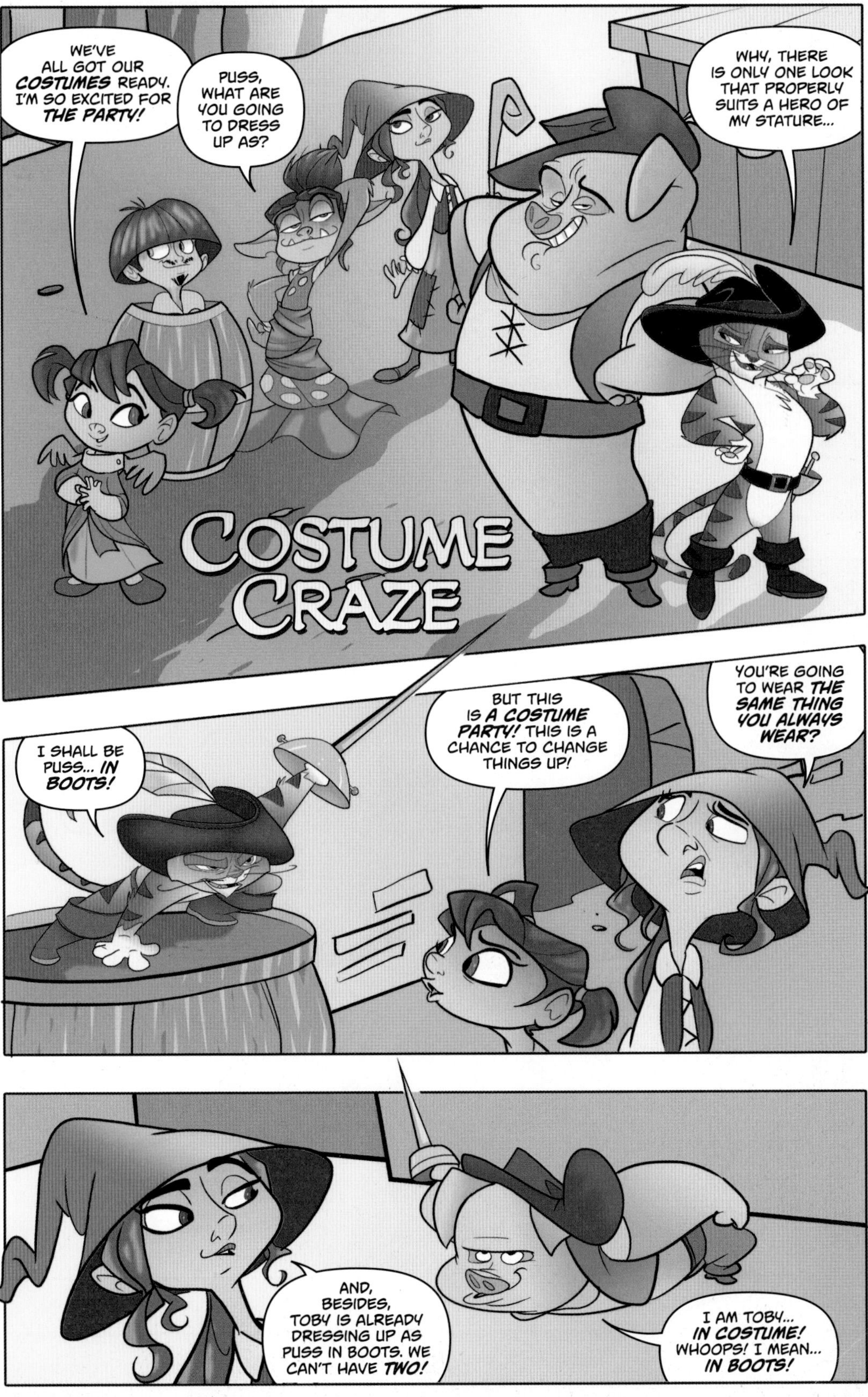

WE'VE ALL GOT OUR COSTUMES READY. I'M SO EXCITED FOR THE PARTY!
PUSS, WHAT ARE YOU GOING TO DRESS UP AS?
WHY, THERE IS ONLY ONE LOOK THAT PROPERLY SUITS A HERO OF MY STATURE...
COSTUME CRAZE
I SHALL BE PUSS... IN BOOTS!
BUT THIS IS A COSTUME PARTY! THIS IS A CHANCE TO CHANGE THINGS UP!
YOU'RE GOING TO WEAR THE SAME THING YOU ALWAYS WEAR?
AND, BESIDES, TOBY IS ALREADY DRESSING UP AS PUSS IN BOOTS. WE CAN'T HAVE TWO!
I AM TOBY... IN COSTUME! WHOOPS! I MEAN... IN BOOTS!

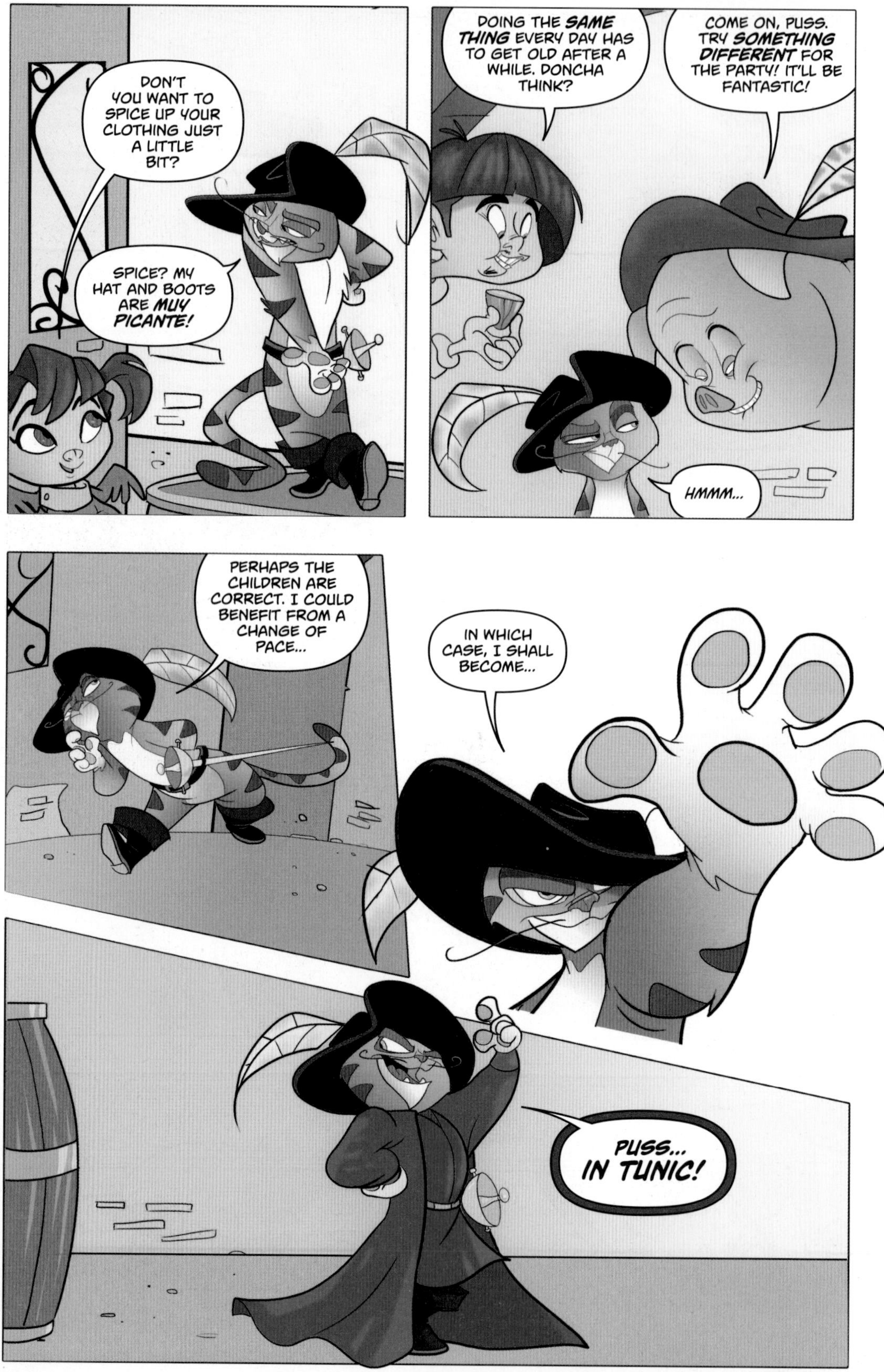
DON'T YOU WANT TO SPICE UP YOUR CLOTHING JUST A LITTLE BIT?
SPICE? MY HAT AND BOOTS ARE MUY PICANTE!
DOING THE SAME THING EVERY DAY HAS TO GET OLD AFTER A WHILE. DONCHA THINK?
COME ON, PUSS. TRY SOMETHING DIFFERENT FOR THE PARTY! IT'LL BE FANTASTIC!
HMMM...
PERHAPS THE CHILDREN ARE CORRECT. I COULD BENEFIT FROM A CHANGE OF PACE...
IN WHICH CASE, I SHALL BECOME...
PUSS... IN TUNIC!

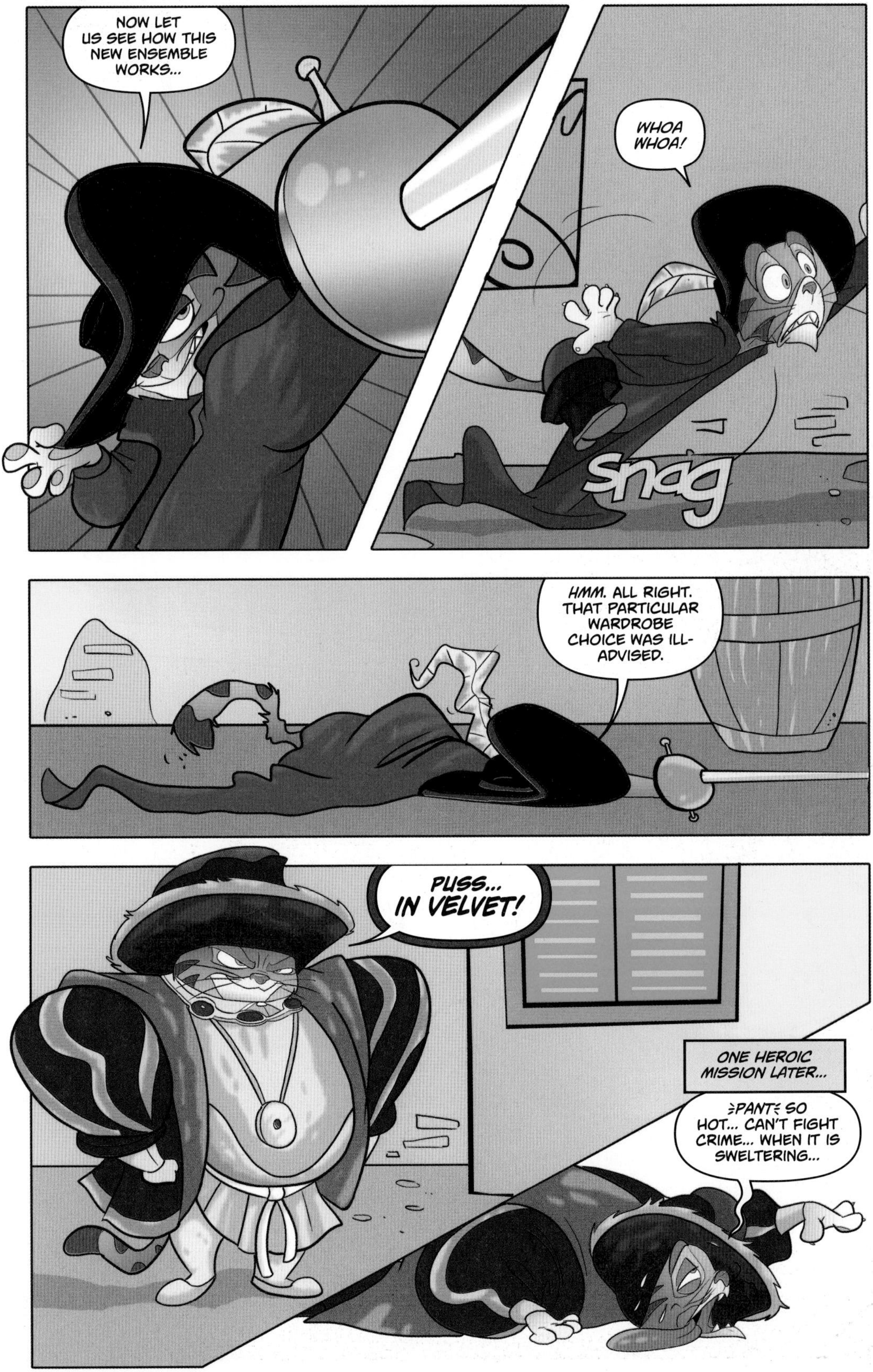
NOW LET US SEE HOW THIS NEW ENSEMBLE WORKS...
WHOA WHOA!
snag
HMM. ALL RIGHT. THAT PARTICULAR WARDROBE CHOICE WAS ILL-ADVISED.
PUSS... IN VELVET!
ONE HEROIC MISSION LATER...
PANT SO HOT... CAN'T FIGHT CRIME... WHEN IT IS SWELTERING...

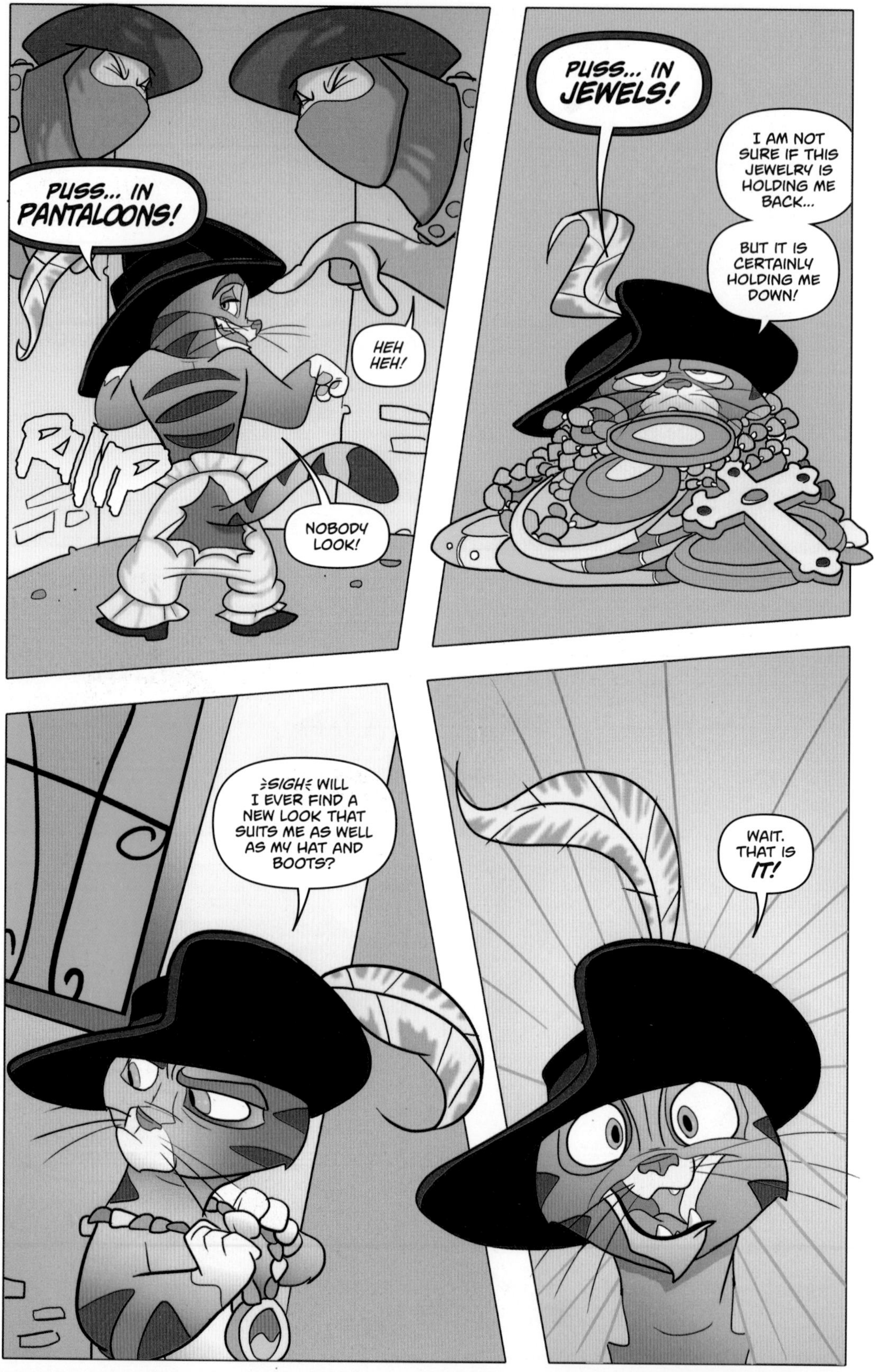
PUSS... IN PANTALOONS!
HEH HEH!
RAIIP
NOBODY LOOK!
PUSS... IN JEWELS!
I AM NOT SURE IF THIS JEWELRY IS HOLDING ME BACK...
BUT IT IS CERTAINLY HOLDING ME DOWN!
SIGH WILL I EVER FIND A NEW LOOK THAT SUITS ME AS WELL AS MY HAT AND BOOTS?
WAIT. THAT IS IT!

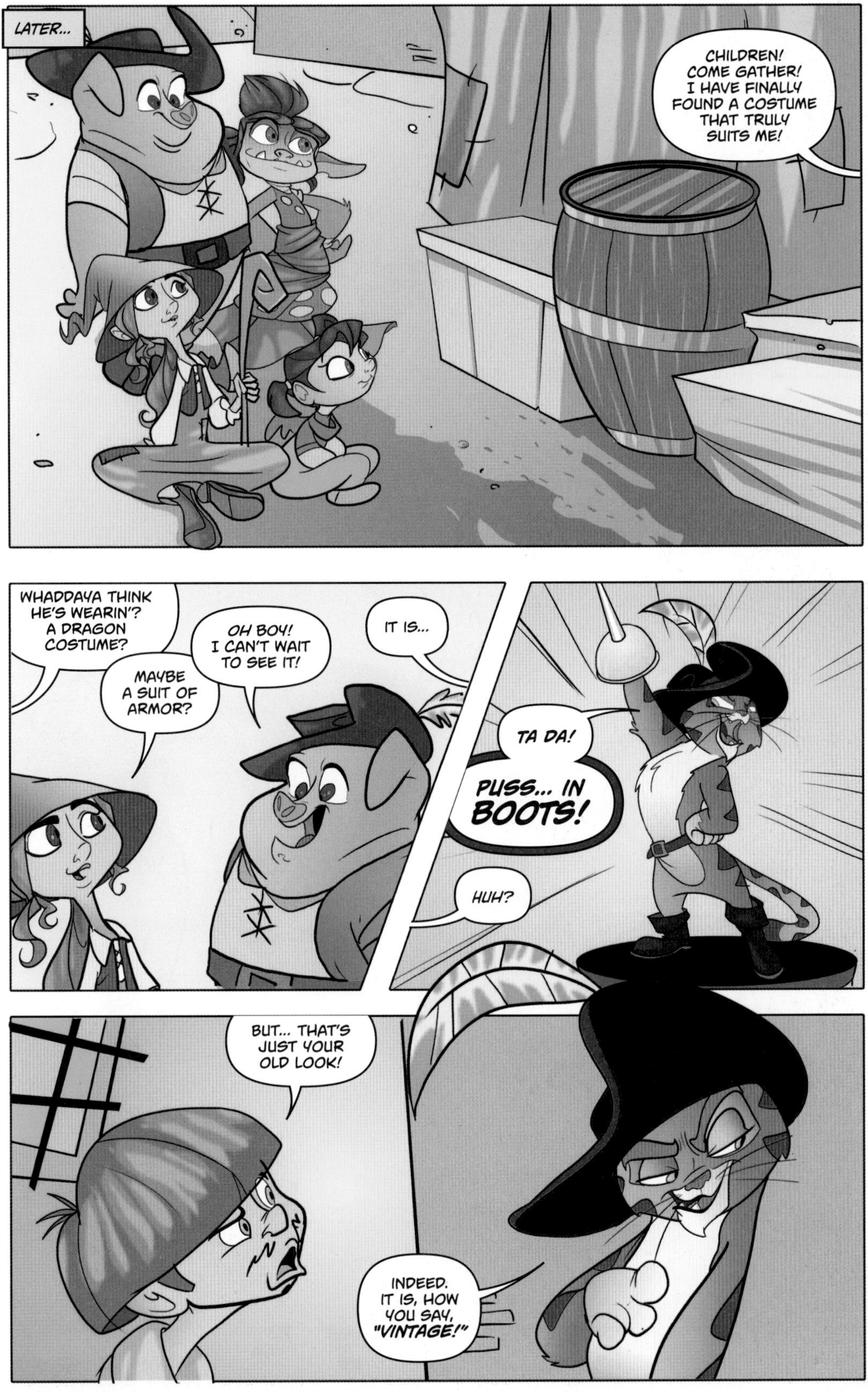
LATER...
CHILDREN! COME GATHER! I HAVE FINALLY FOUND A COSTUME THAT TRULY SUITS ME!
WHADDAYA THINK HE'S WEARIN'? A DRAGON COSTUME?
MAYBE A SUIT OF ARMOR?
OH BOY! I CAN'T WAIT TO SEE IT!
IT IS...
TA DA!
PUSS... IN BOOTS!
HUH?
BUT... THAT'S JUST YOUR OLD LOOK!
INDEED. IT IS, HOW YOU SAY, "VINTAGE!"

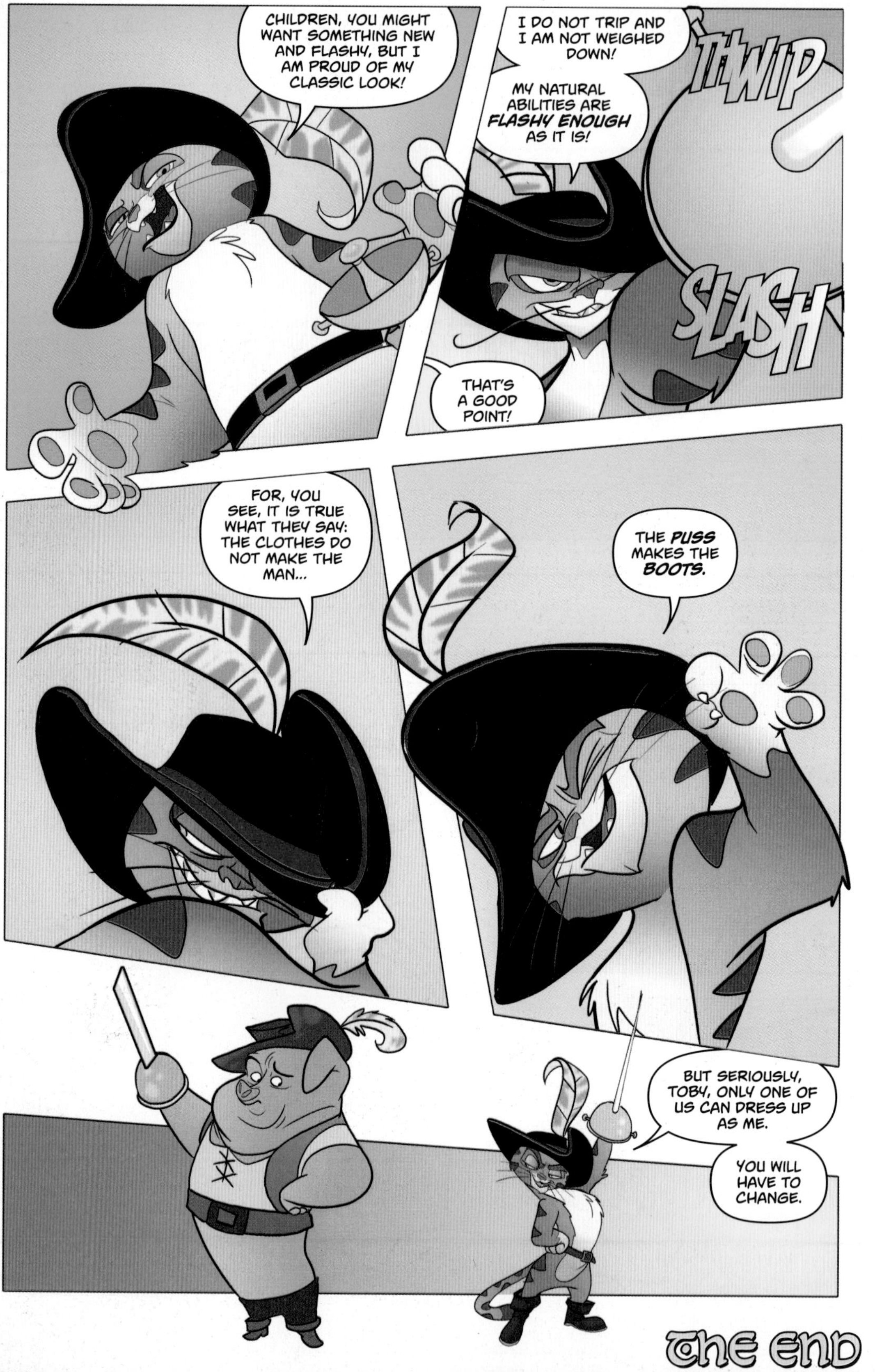
CHILDREN, YOU MIGHT WANT SOMETHING NEW AND FLASHY, BUT I AM PROUD OF MY CLASSIC LOOK!
I DO NOT TRIP AND I AM NOT WEIGHED DOWN!
MY NATURAL ABILITIES ARE FLASHY ENOUGH AS IT IS!
THWIP
SLASH
THAT'S A GOOD POINT!
FOR, YOU SEE, IT IS TRUE WHAT THEY SAY: THE CLOTHES DO NOT MAKE THE MAN...
THE PUSS MAKES THE BOOTS.
BUT SERIOUSLY, TOBY, ONLY ONE OF US CAN DRESS UP AS ME.
YOU WILL HAVE TO CHANGE.
THE END

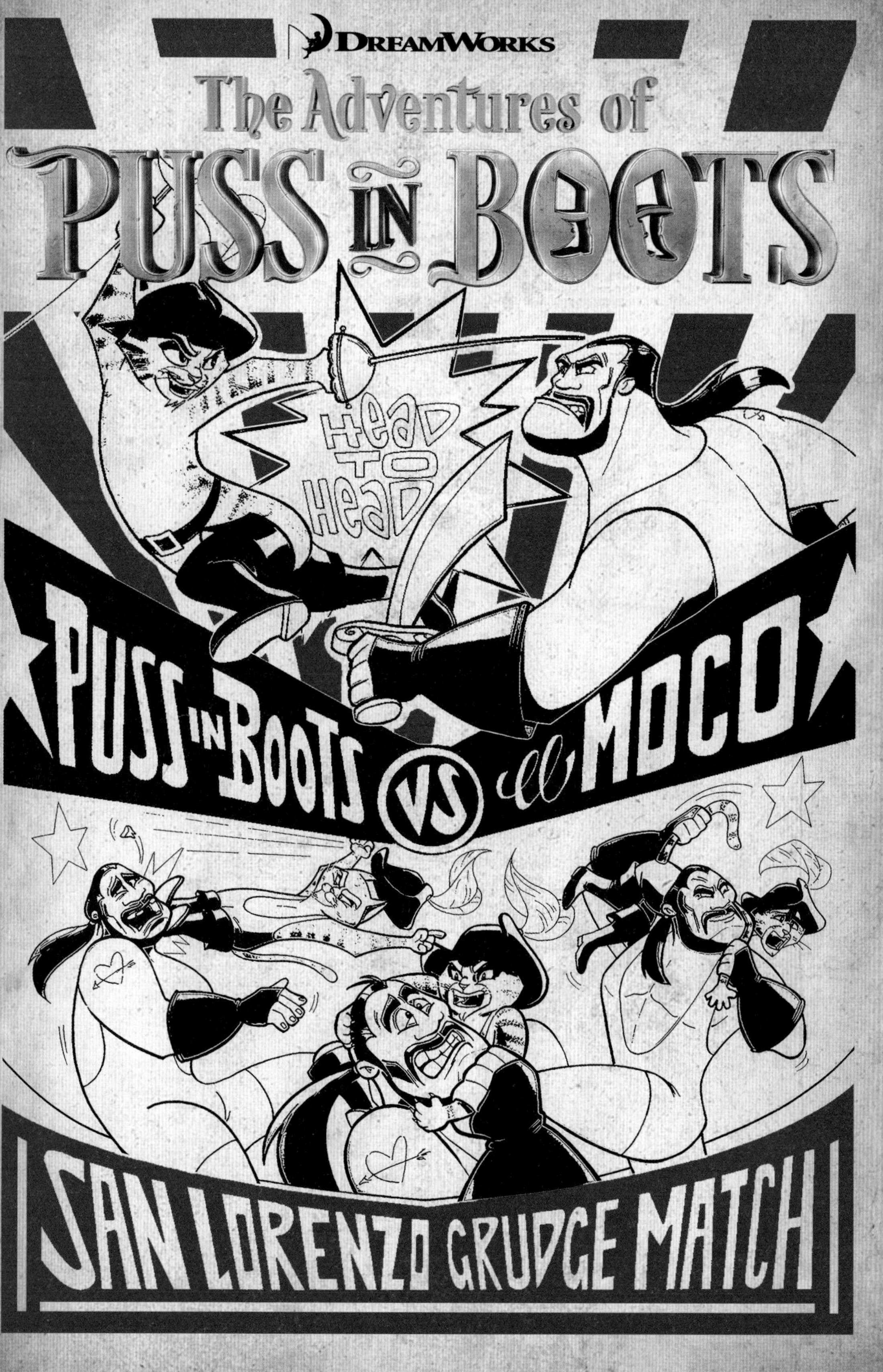
DreamWorks
The Adventures of
PUSS IN BOOTS
HEAD TO HEAD
PUSS IN BOOTS VS el MOCO
SAN LORENZO GRUDGE MATCH

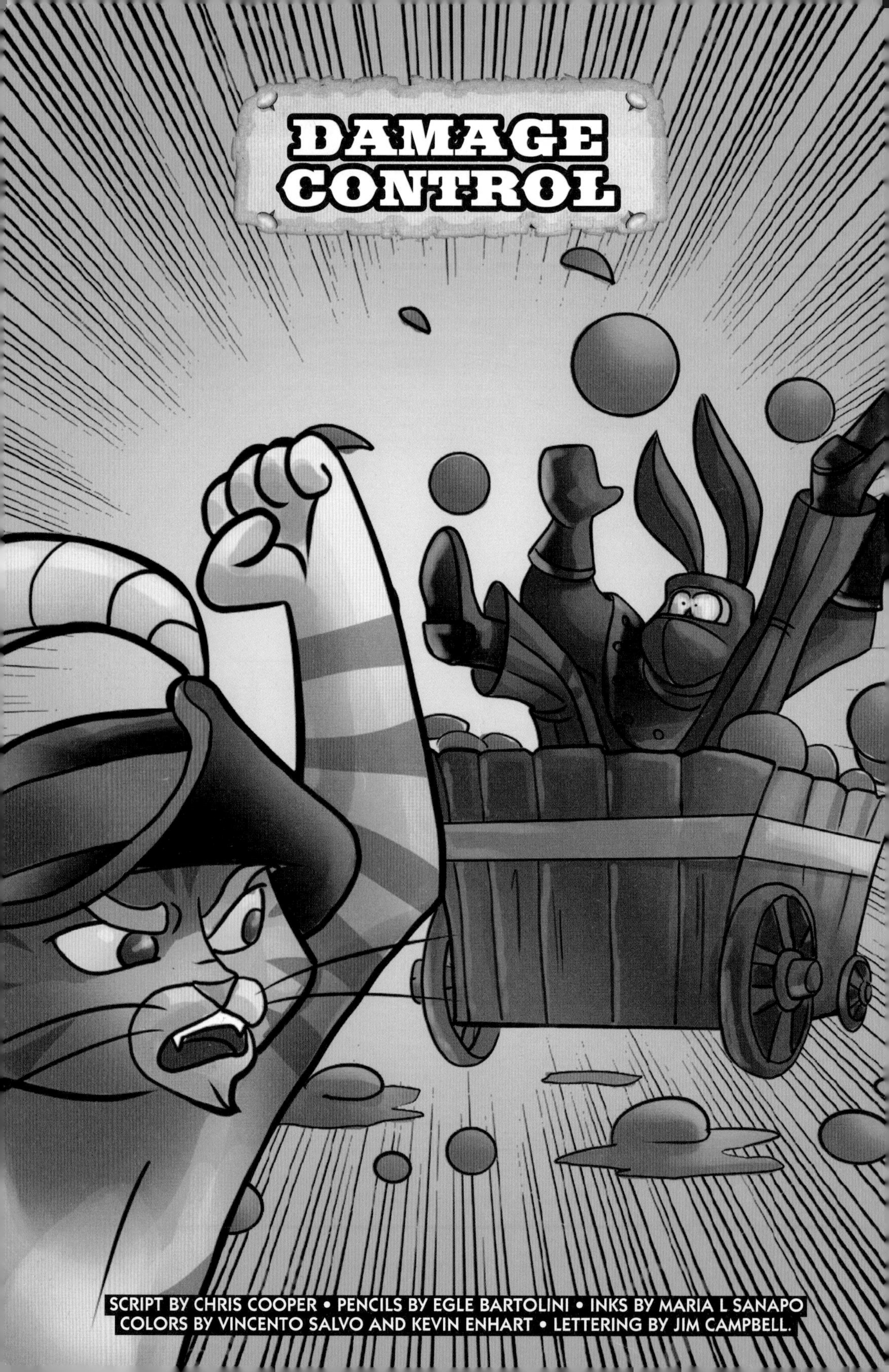
DAMAGE CONTROL
SCRIPT BY CHRIS COOPER • PENCILS BY EGLE BARTOLINI • INKS BY MARIA L SANAPO
COLORS BY VINCENTO SALVO AND KEVIN ENHART • LETTERING BY JIM CAMPBELL.

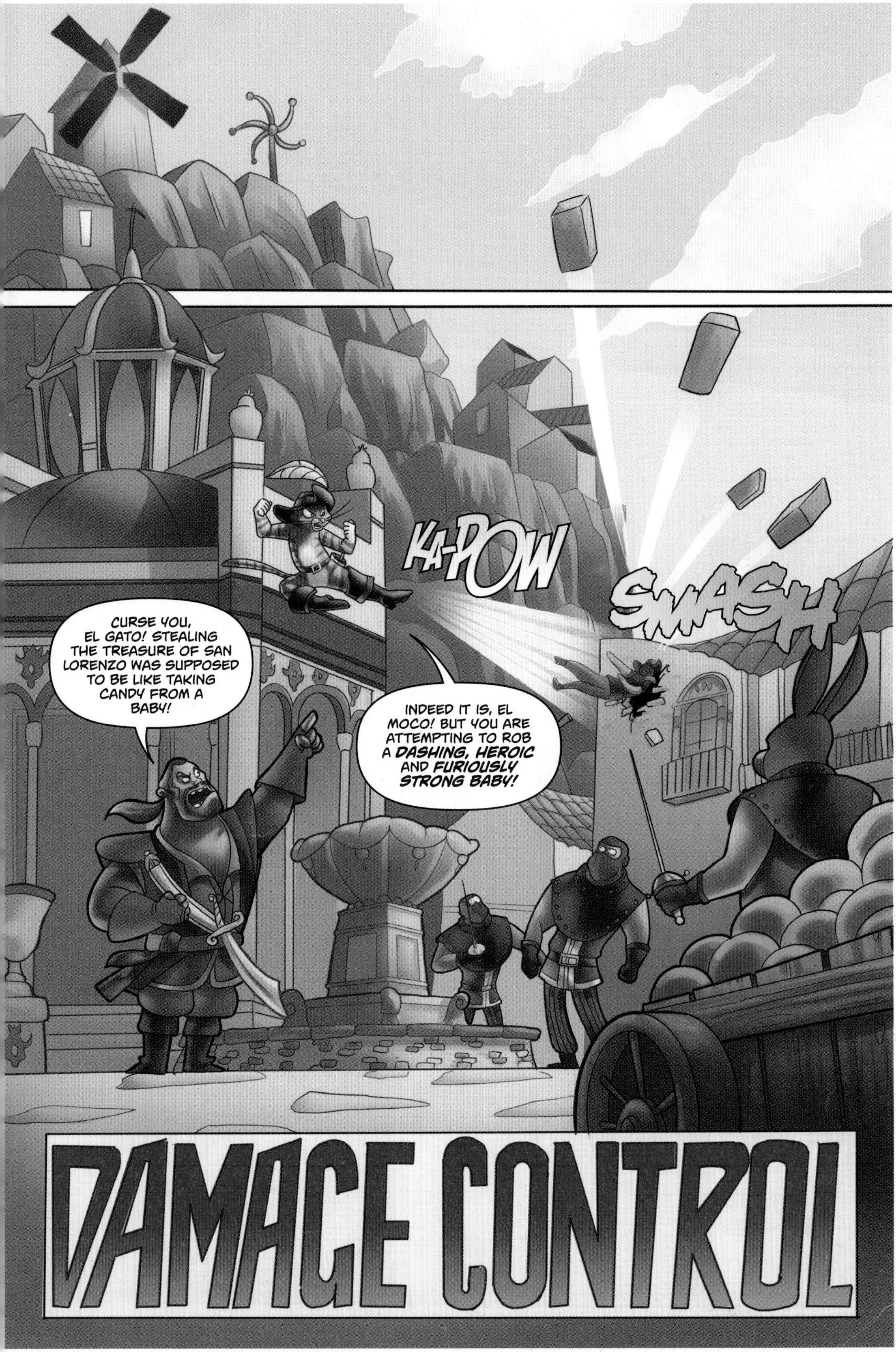
KA-POW
SMASH
CURSE YOU, EL GATO! STEALING THE TREASURE OF SAN LORENZO WAS SUPPOSED TO BE LIKE TAKING CANDY FROM A BABY!
INDEED IT IS, EL MOCO! BUT YOU ARE ATTEMPTING TO ROB A DASHING, HEROIC AND FURIOUSLY STRONG BABY!
DAMAGE CONTROL

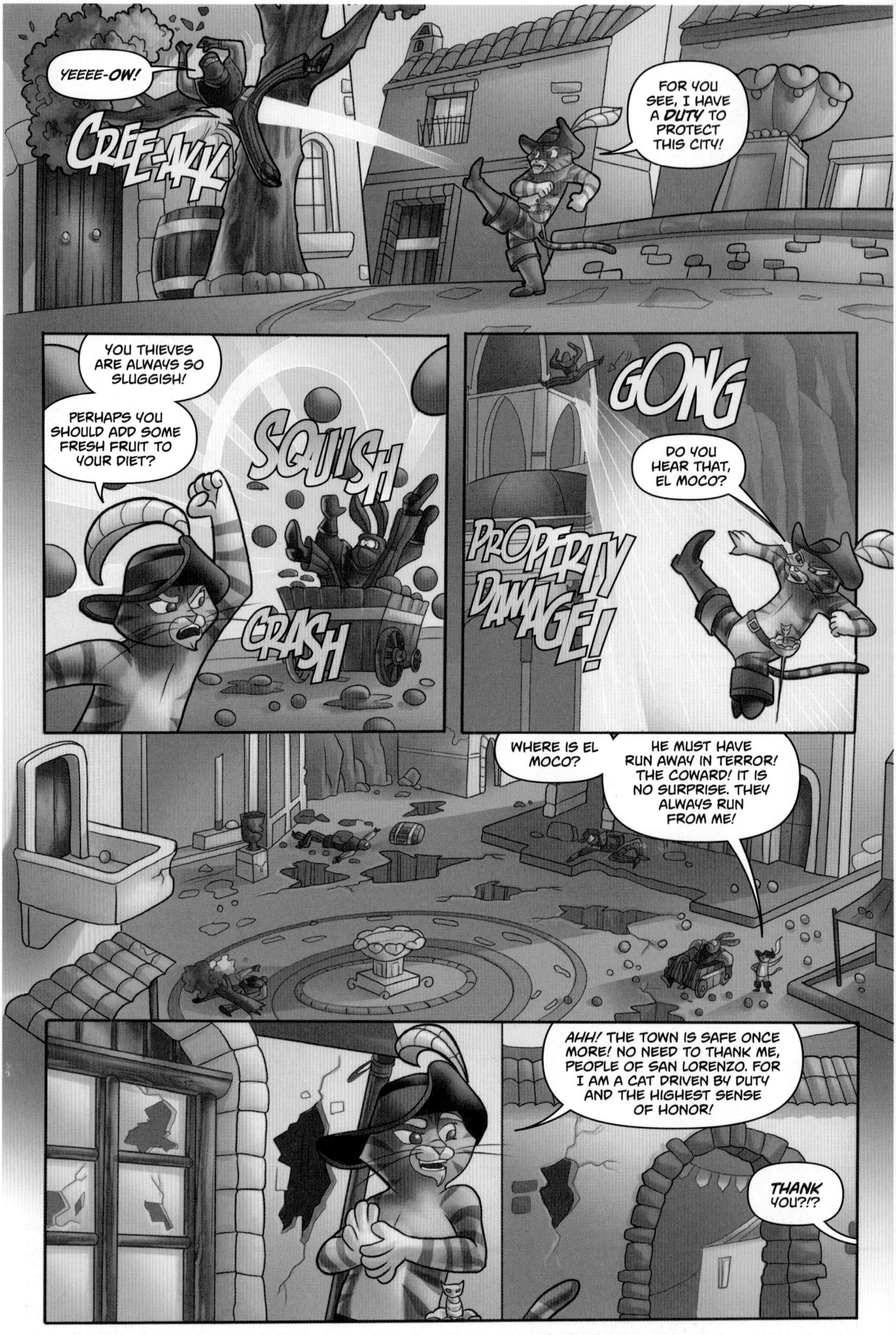
YEEEE-OW!
CREE-AKK
FOR YOU SEE, I HAVE A DUTY TO PROTECT THIS CITY!
YOU THIEVES ARE ALWAYS SO SLUGGISH!
PERHAPS YOU SHOULD ADD SOME FRESH FRUIT TO YOUR DIET?
SQUISH
CRASH
GONG
DO YOU HEAR THAT, EL MOCO?
PROPERTY DAMAGE!
WHERE IS EL MOCO?
HE MUST HAVE RUN AWAY IN TERROR! THE COWARD! IT IS NO SURPRISE. THEY ALWAYS RUN FROM ME!
AHH! THE TOWN IS SAFE ONCE MORE! NO NEED TO THANK ME, PEOPLE OF SAN LORENZO. FOR I AM A CAT DRIVEN BY DUTY AND THE HIGHEST SENSE OF HONOR!
THANK YOU?!?

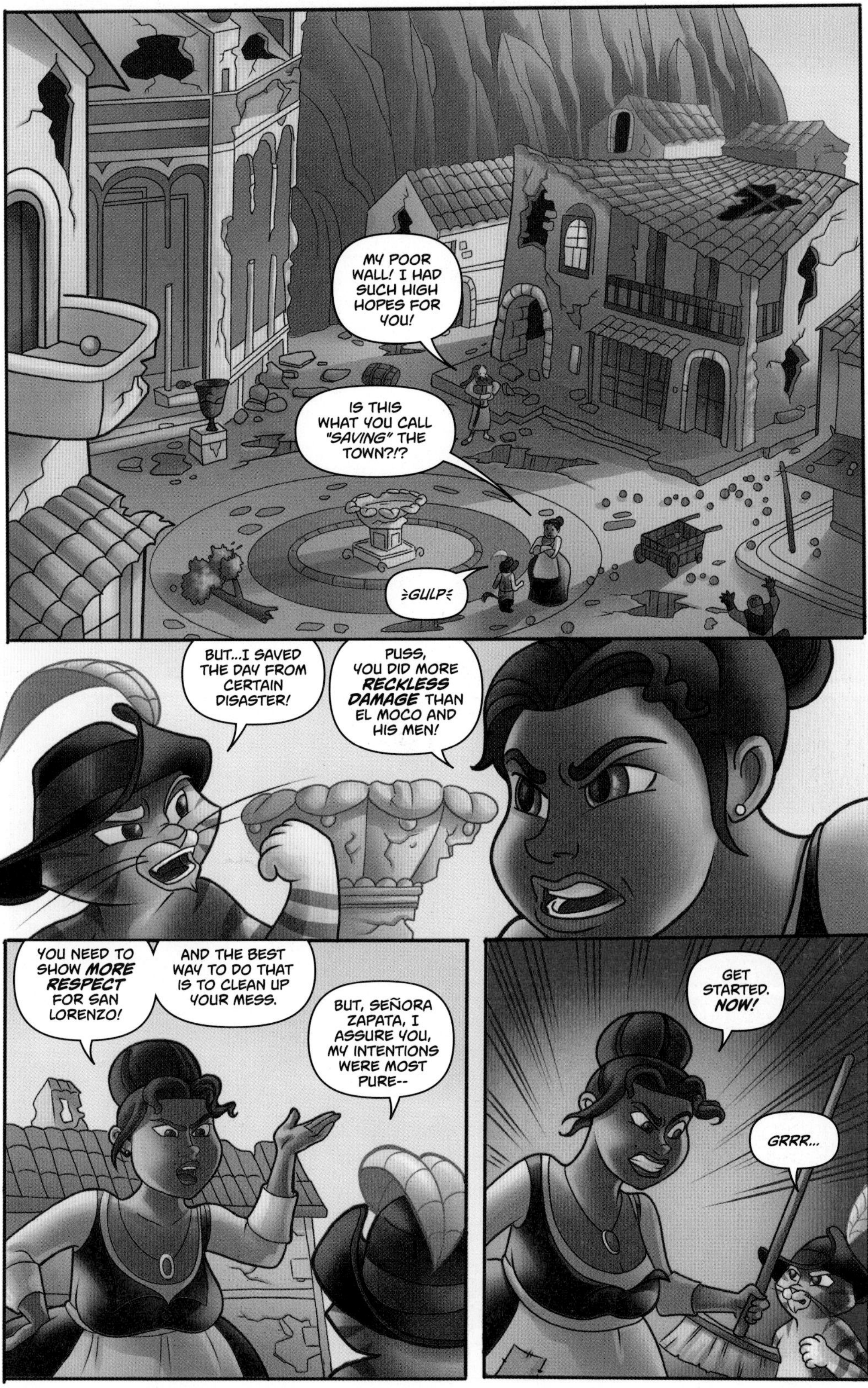
MY POOR WALL! I HAD SUCH HIGH HOPES FOR YOU!
IS THIS WHAT YOU CALL "SAVING" THE TOWN?!?
GULP
BUT...I SAVED THE DAY FROM CERTAIN DISASTER!
PUSS, YOU DID MORE RECKLESS DAMAGE THAN EL MOCO AND HIS MEN!
YOU NEED TO SHOW MORE RESPECT FOR SAN LORENZO!
AND THE BEST WAY TO DO THAT IS TO CLEAN UP YOUR MESS.
BUT, SEÑORA ZAPATA, I ASSURE YOU, MY INTENTIONS WERE MOST PURE--
GET STARTED. NOW!
GRRR...

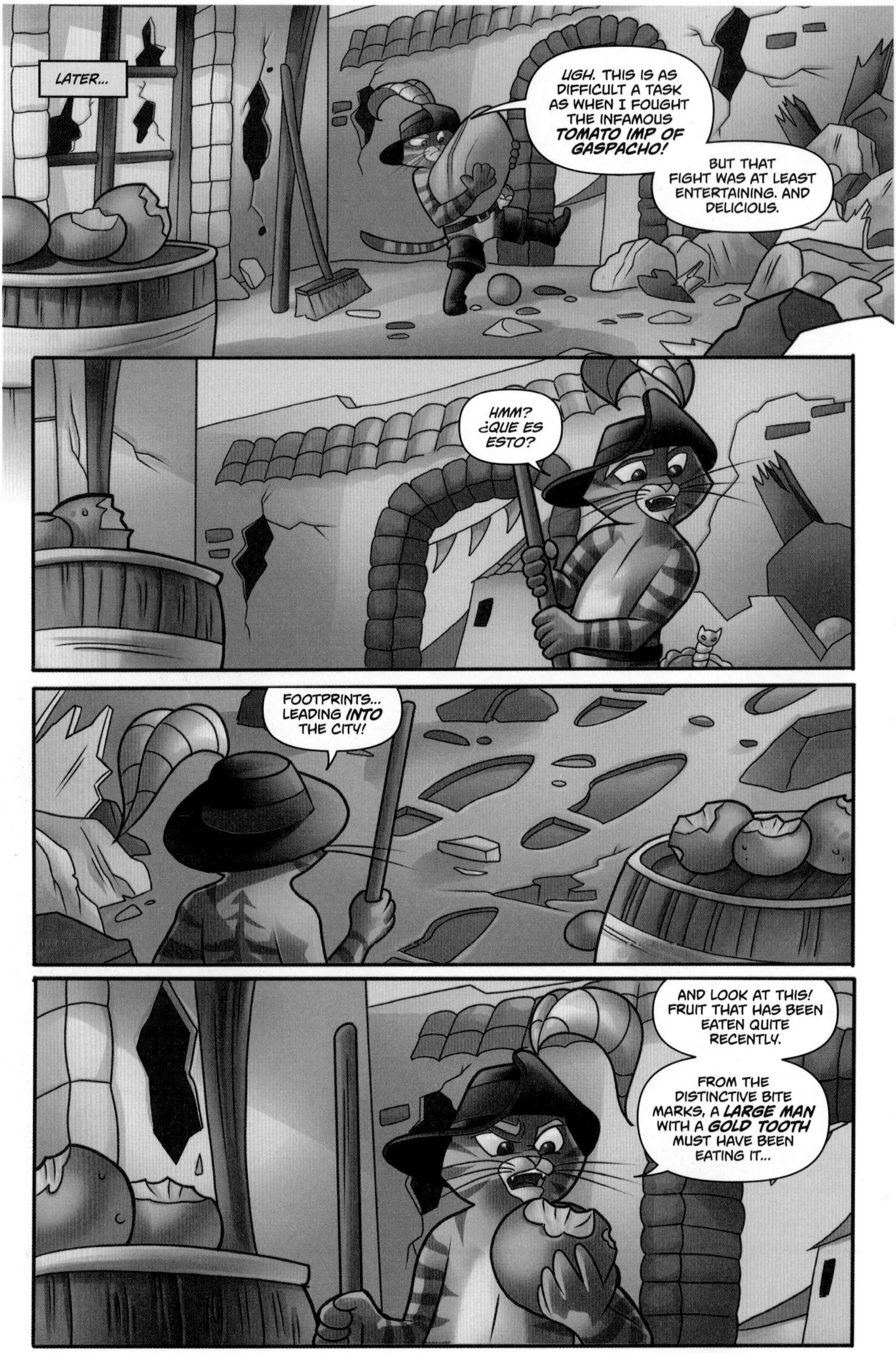
LATER...
UGH. THIS IS AS DIFFICULT A TASK AS WHEN I FOUGHT THE INFAMOUS ***TOMATO IMP OF GASPACHO!***
BUT THAT FIGHT WAS AT LEAST ENTERTAINING. AND DELICIOUS.
HMM? ¿QUE ES ESTO?
FOOTPRINTS... LEADING ***INTO*** THE CITY!
AND LOOK AT THIS! FRUIT THAT HAS BEEN EATEN QUITE RECENTLY.
FROM THE DISTINCTIVE BITE MARKS, A ***LARGE MAN*** WITH A ***GOLD TOOTH*** MUST HAVE BEEN EATING IT...

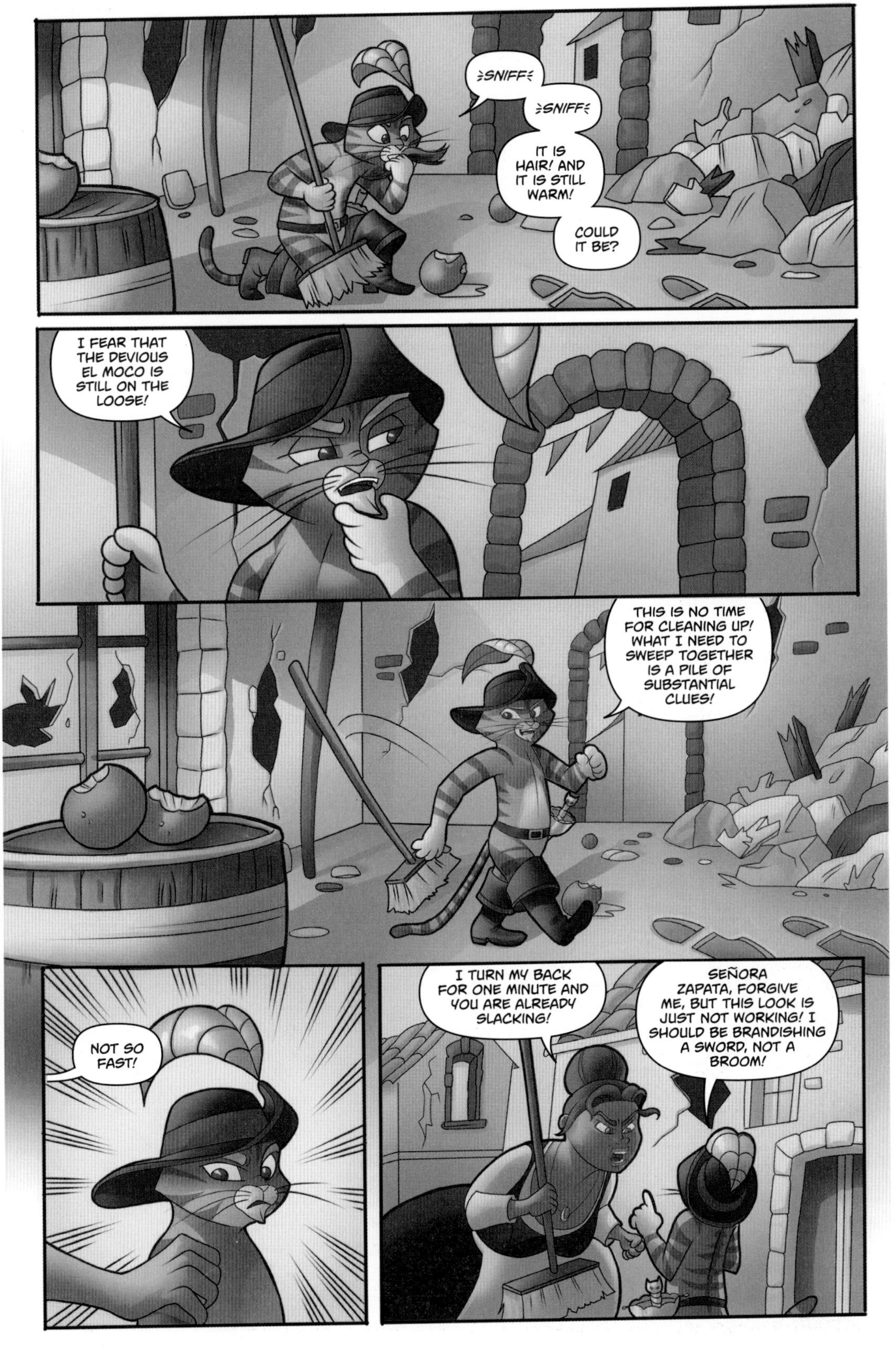

SNIFF
SNIFF
IT IS HAIR! AND IT IS STILL WARM!
COULD IT BE?
I FEAR THAT THE DEVIOUS EL MOCO IS STILL ON THE LOOSE!
THIS IS NO TIME FOR CLEANING UP! WHAT I NEED TO SWEEP TOGETHER IS A PILE OF SUBSTANTIAL CLUES!
NOT SO FAST!
I TURN MY BACK FOR ONE MINUTE AND YOU ARE ALREADY SLACKING!
SEÑORA ZAPATA, FORGIVE ME, BUT THIS LOOK IS JUST NOT WORKING! I SHOULD BE BRANDISHING A SWORD, NOT A BROOM!

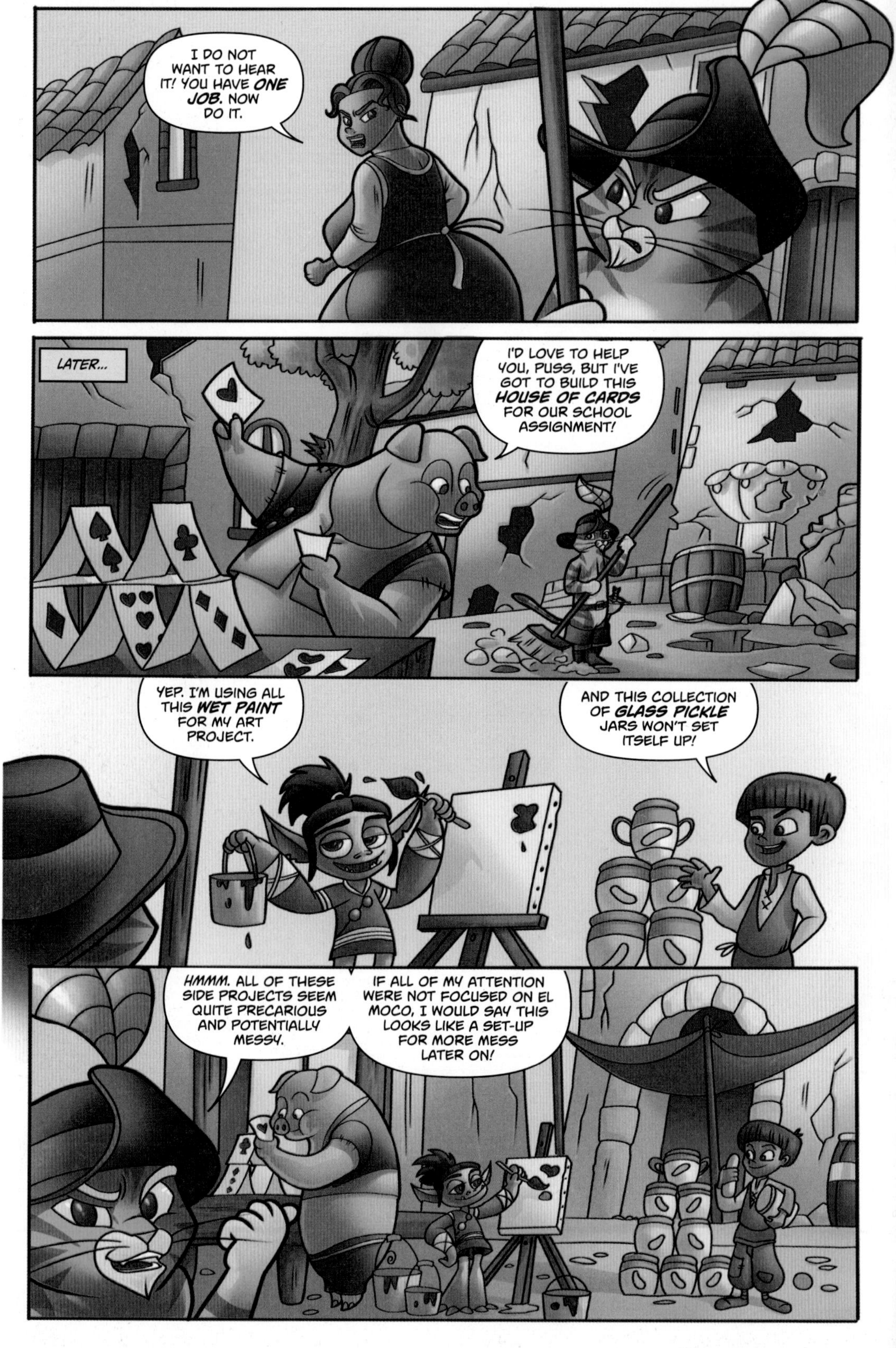
I DO NOT WANT TO HEAR IT! YOU HAVE ONE JOB. NOW DO IT.
LATER...
I'D LOVE TO HELP YOU, PUSS, BUT I'VE GOT TO BUILD THIS HOUSE OF CARDS FOR OUR SCHOOL ASSIGNMENT!
YEP. I'M USING ALL THIS WET PAINT FOR MY ART PROJECT.
AND THIS COLLECTION OF GLASS PICKLE JARS WON'T SET ITSELF UP!
HMMM. ALL OF THESE SIDE PROJECTS SEEM QUITE PRECARIOUS AND POTENTIALLY MESSY.
IF ALL OF MY ATTENTION WERE NOT FOCUSED ON EL MOCO, I WOULD SAY THIS LOOKS LIKE A SET-UP FOR MORE MESS LATER ON!

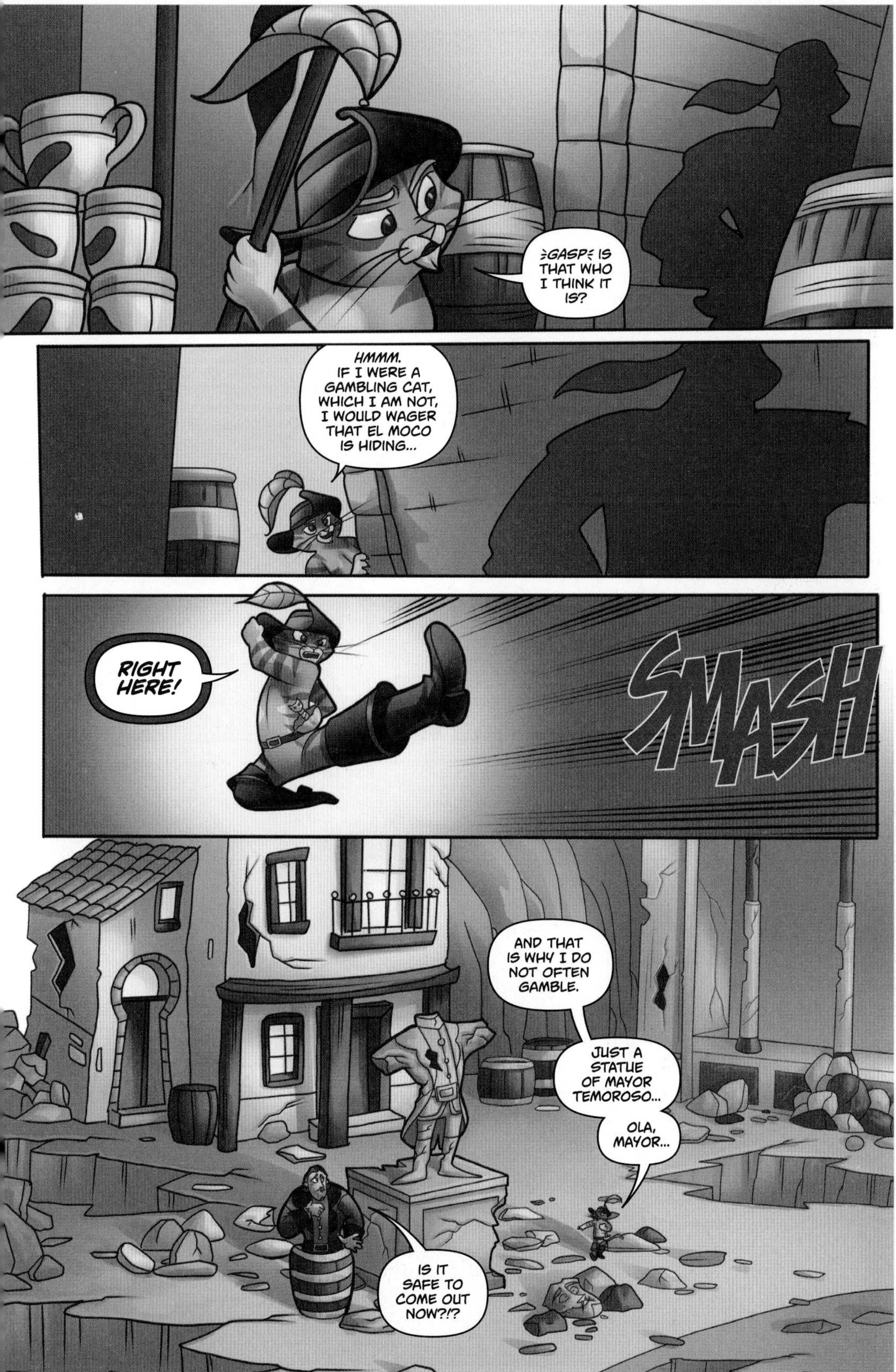

⪢GASP⪡ IS THAT WHO I THINK IT IS?
HMMM. IF I WERE A GAMBLING CAT, WHICH I AM NOT, I WOULD WAGER THAT EL MOCO IS HIDING...
RIGHT HERE!
SMASH
AND THAT IS WHY I DO NOT OFTEN GAMBLE.
JUST A STATUE OF MAYOR TEMOROSO...
OLA, MAYOR...
IS IT SAFE TO COME OUT NOW?!?

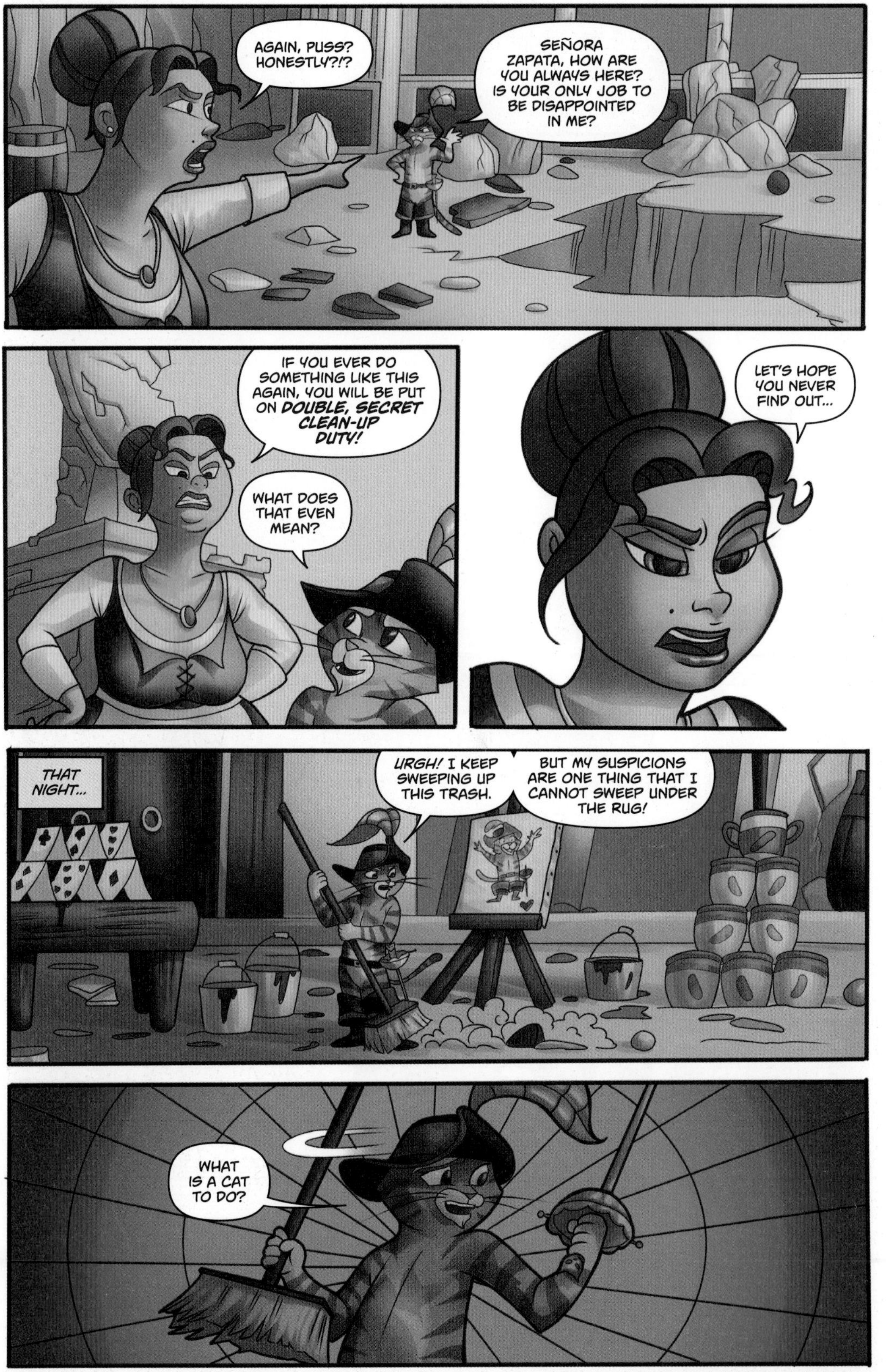
AGAIN, PUSS? HONESTLY?!?
SEÑORA ZAPATA, HOW ARE YOU ALWAYS HERE? IS YOUR ONLY JOB TO BE DISAPPOINTED IN ME?
IF YOU EVER DO SOMETHING LIKE THIS AGAIN, YOU WILL BE PUT ON *DOUBLE, SECRET CLEAN-UP DUTY!*
WHAT DOES THAT EVEN MEAN?
LET'S HOPE YOU NEVER FIND OUT...
THAT NIGHT...
URGH! I KEEP SWEEPING UP THIS TRASH.
BUT MY SUSPICIONS ARE ONE THING THAT I CANNOT SWEEP UNDER THE RUG!
WHAT IS A CAT TO DO?

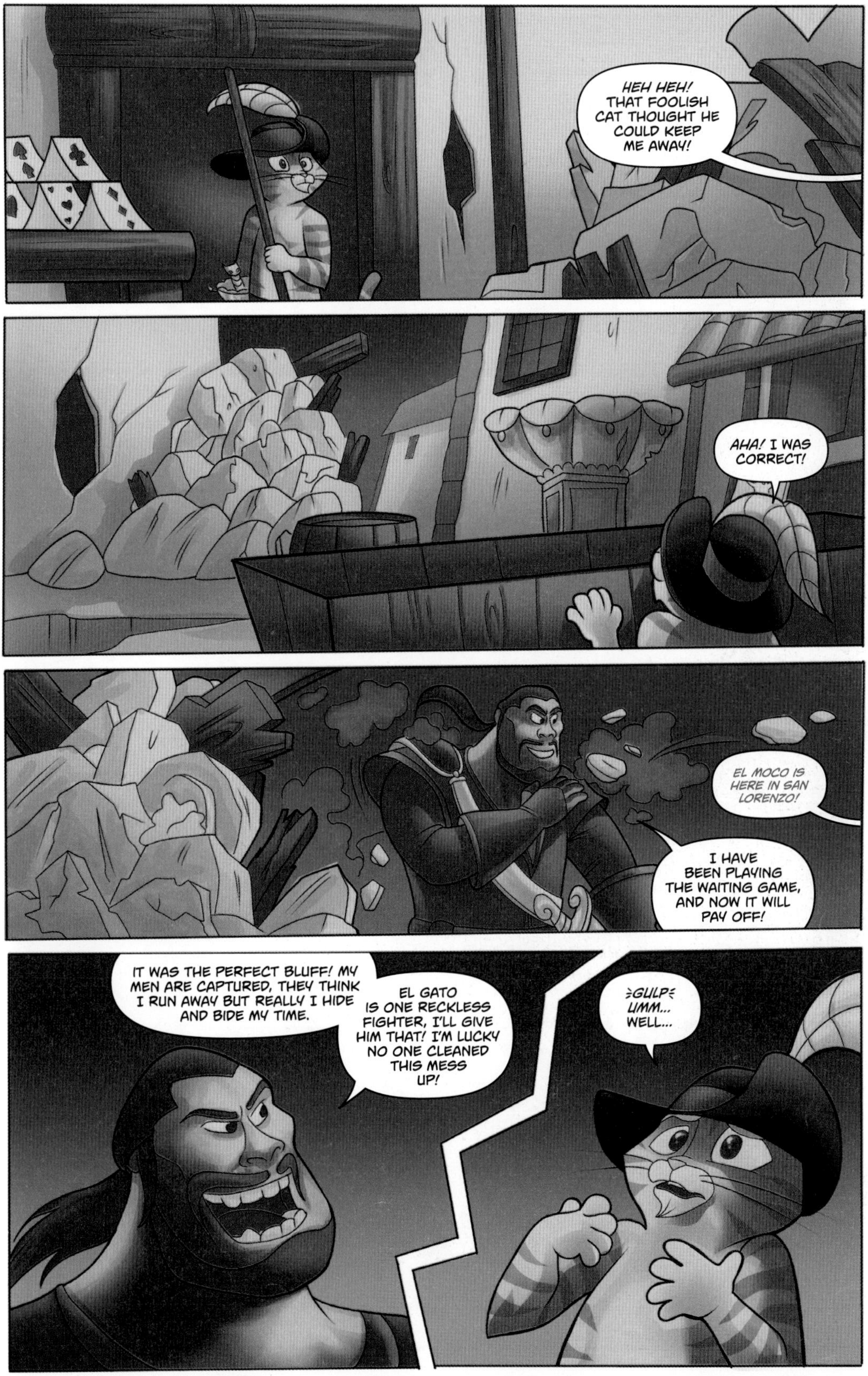
HEH HEH! THAT FOOLISH CAT THOUGHT HE COULD KEEP ME AWAY!
AHA! I WAS CORRECT!
EL MOCO IS HERE IN SAN LORENZO!
I HAVE BEEN PLAYING THE WAITING GAME, AND NOW IT WILL PAY OFF!
IT WAS THE PERFECT BLUFF! MY MEN ARE CAPTURED, THEY THINK I RUN AWAY BUT REALLY I HIDE AND BIDE MY TIME.
EL GATO IS ONE RECKLESS FIGHTER, I'LL GIVE HIM THAT! I'M LUCKY NO ONE CLEANED THIS MESS UP!
GULP UMM... WELL...

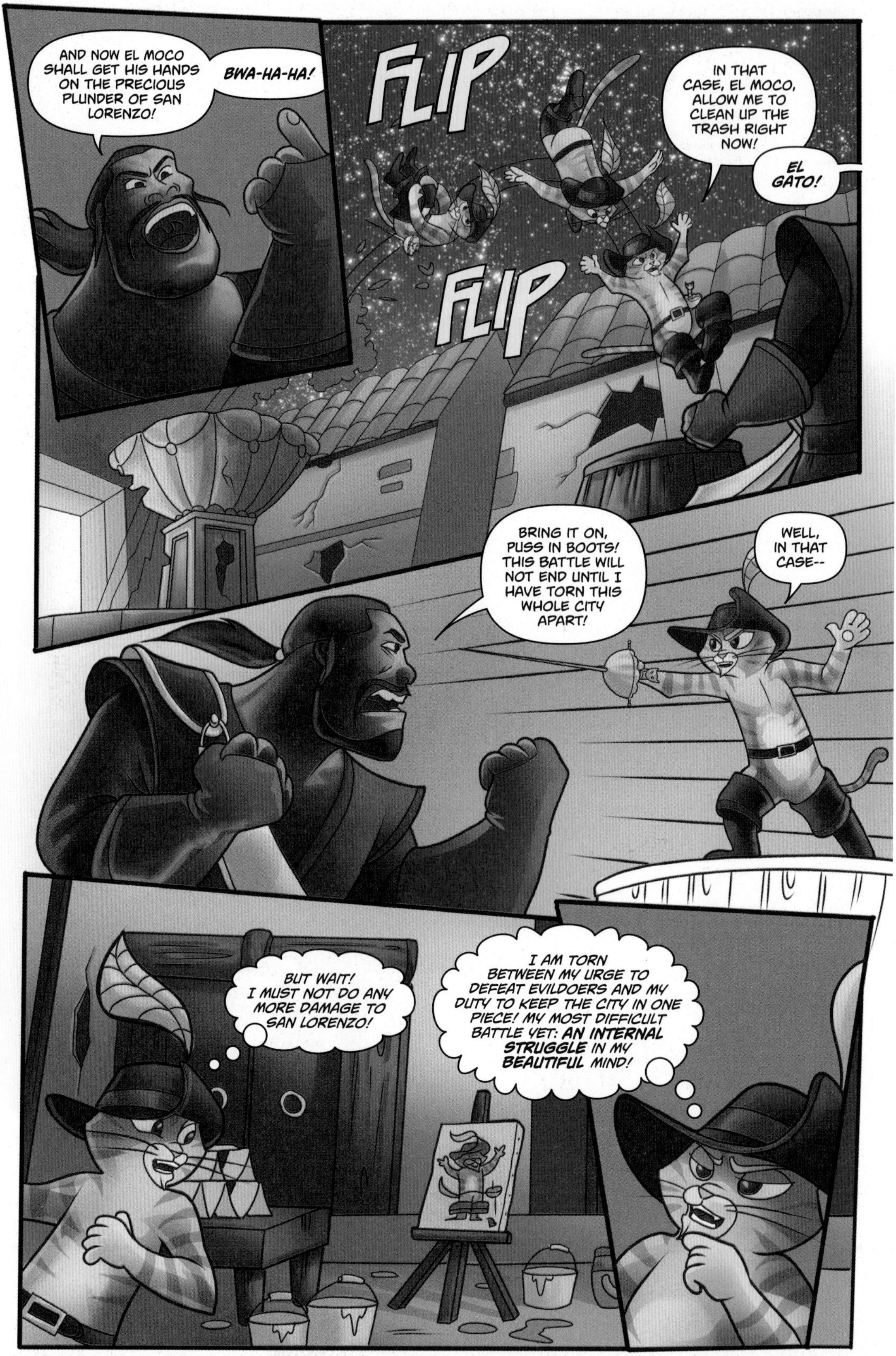
AND NOW EL MOCO SHALL GET HIS HANDS ON THE PRECIOUS PLUNDER OF SAN LORENZO!
BWA-HA-HA!
FLIP
FLIP
IN THAT CASE, EL MOCO, ALLOW ME TO CLEAN UP THE TRASH RIGHT NOW!
EL GATO!
BRING IT ON, PUSS IN BOOTS! THIS BATTLE WILL NOT END UNTIL I HAVE TORN THIS WHOLE CITY APART!
WELL, IN THAT CASE--
BUT WAIT! I MUST NOT DO ANY MORE DAMAGE TO SAN LORENZO!
I AM TORN BETWEEN MY URGE TO DEFEAT EVILDOERS AND MY DUTY TO KEEP THE CITY IN ONE PIECE! MY MOST DIFFICULT BATTLE YET: AN INTERNAL STRUGGLE IN MY BEAUTIFUL MIND!

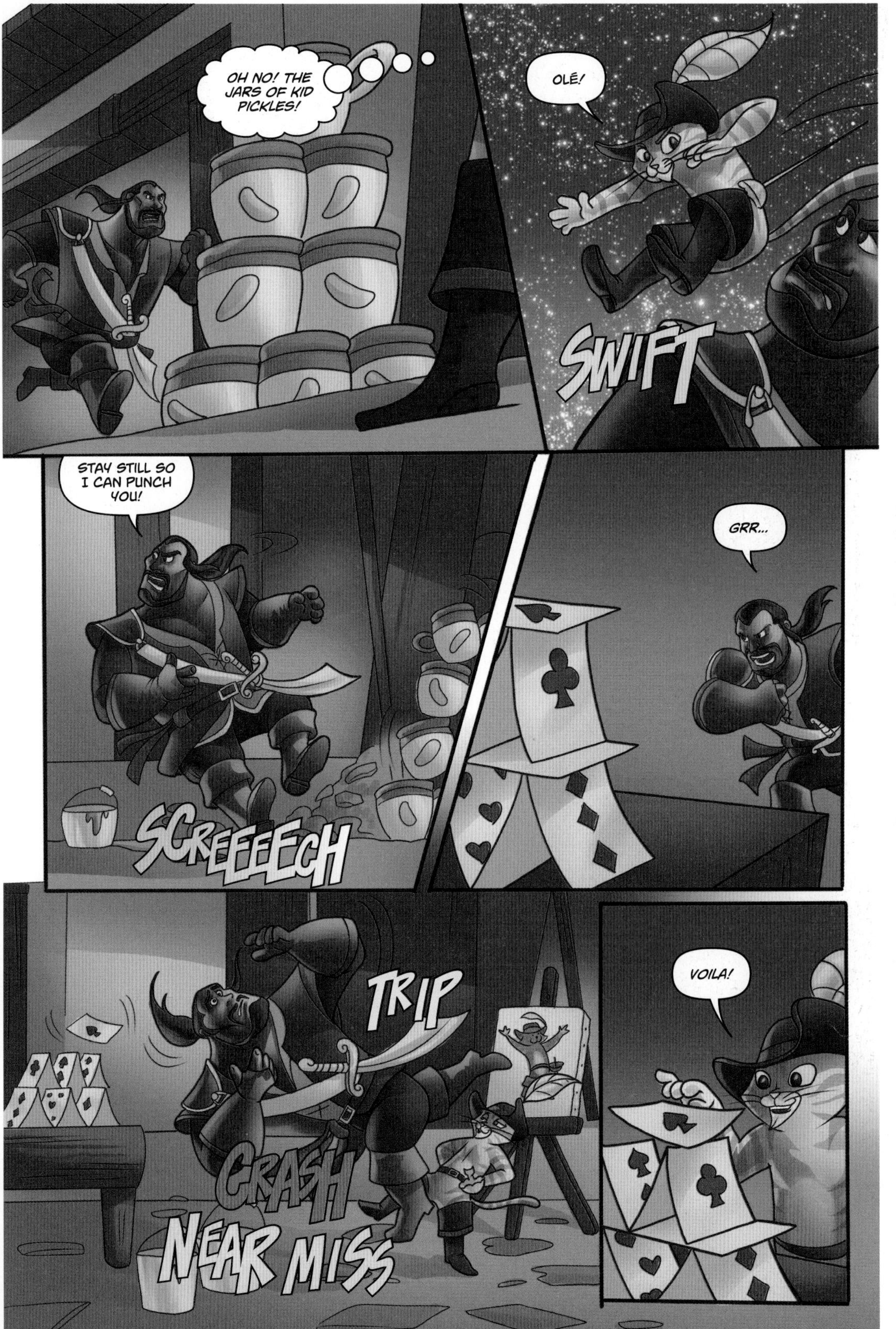
OH NO! THE JARS OF KID PICKLES!
OLÉ!
SWIFT
STAY STILL SO I CAN PUNCH YOU!
SCREEEEECH
GRR...
TRIP
CRASH
NEAR MISS
VOILA!

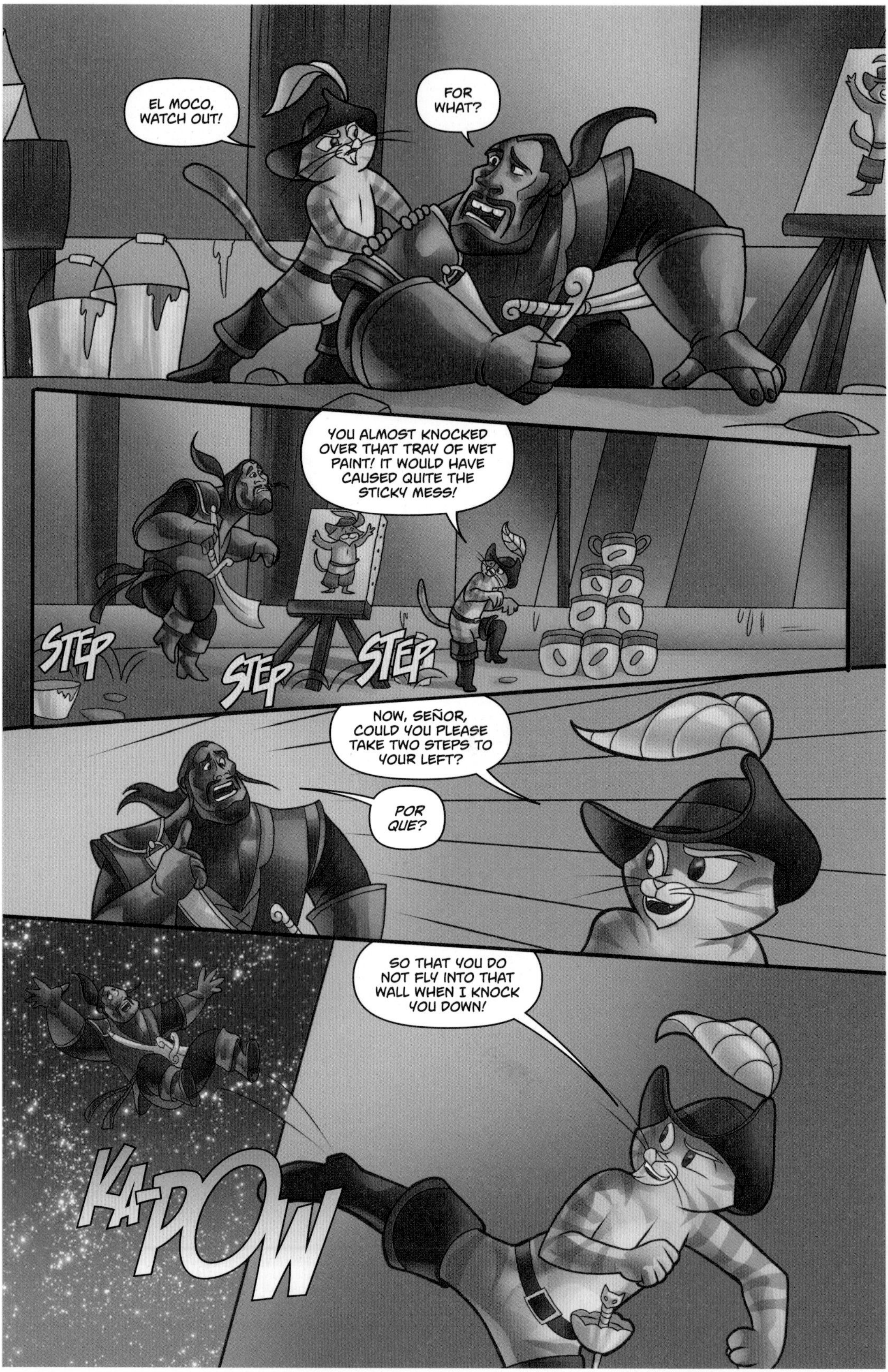
EL MOCO, WATCH OUT!
FOR WHAT?
YOU ALMOST KNOCKED OVER THAT TRAY OF WET PAINT! IT WOULD HAVE CAUSED QUITE THE STICKY MESS!
STEP
STEP
STEP
NOW, SEÑOR, COULD YOU PLEASE TAKE TWO STEPS TO YOUR LEFT?
POR QUE?
SO THAT YOU DO NOT FLY INTO THAT WALL WHEN I KNOCK YOU DOWN!
KA-POW

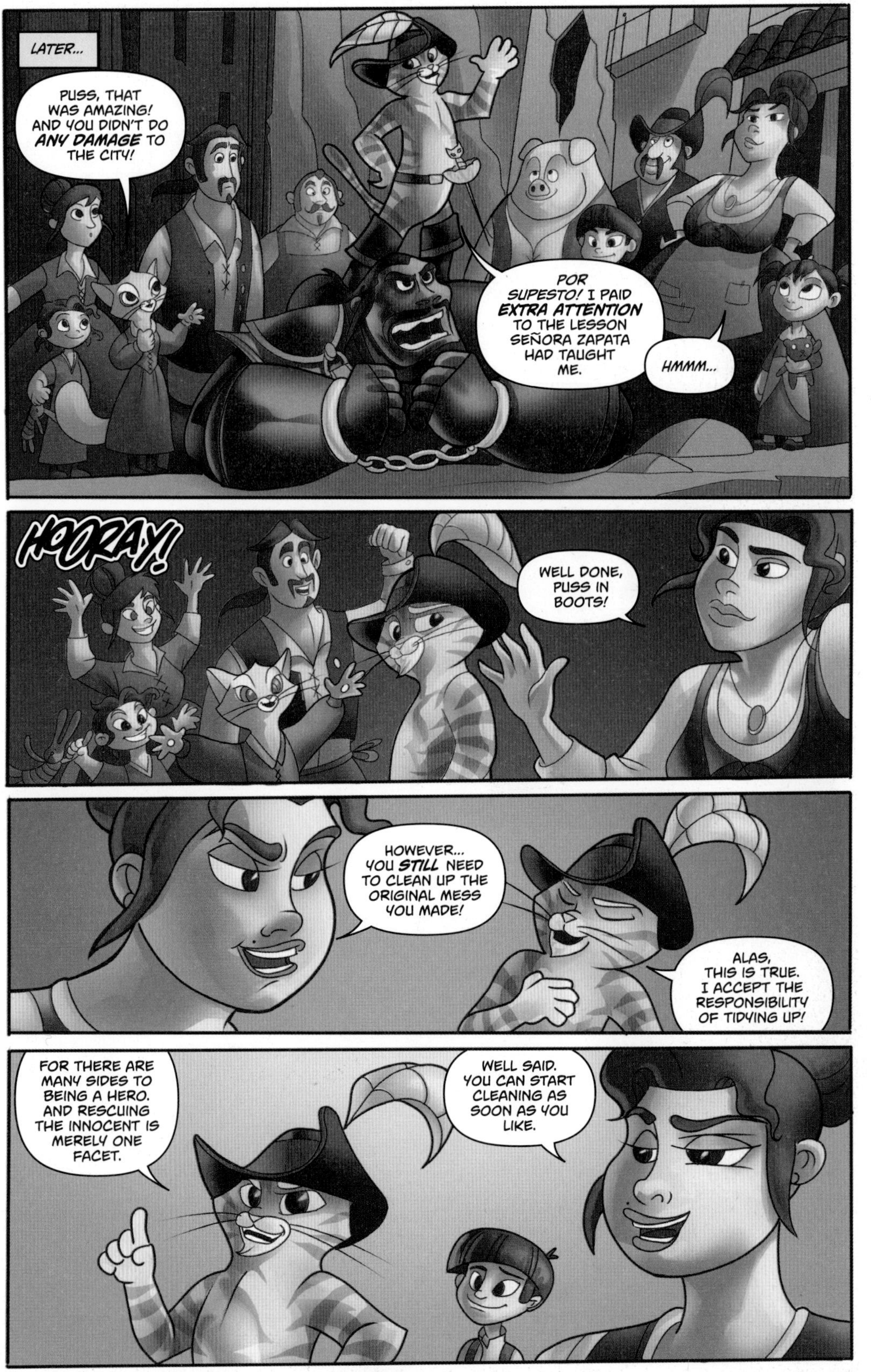
LATER...
PUSS, THAT WAS AMAZING! AND YOU DIDN'T DO ANY DAMAGE TO THE CITY!
POR SUPESTO! I PAID EXTRA ATTENTION TO THE LESSON SEÑORA ZAPATA HAD TAUGHT ME.
HMMM...
HOORAY!
WELL DONE, PUSS IN BOOTS!
HOWEVER... YOU STILL NEED TO CLEAN UP THE ORIGINAL MESS YOU MADE!
ALAS, THIS IS TRUE. I ACCEPT THE RESPONSIBILITY OF TIDYING UP!
FOR THERE ARE MANY SIDES TO BEING A HERO. AND RESCUING THE INNOCENT IS MERELY ONE FACET.
WELL SAID. YOU CAN START CLEANING AS SOON AS YOU LIKE.

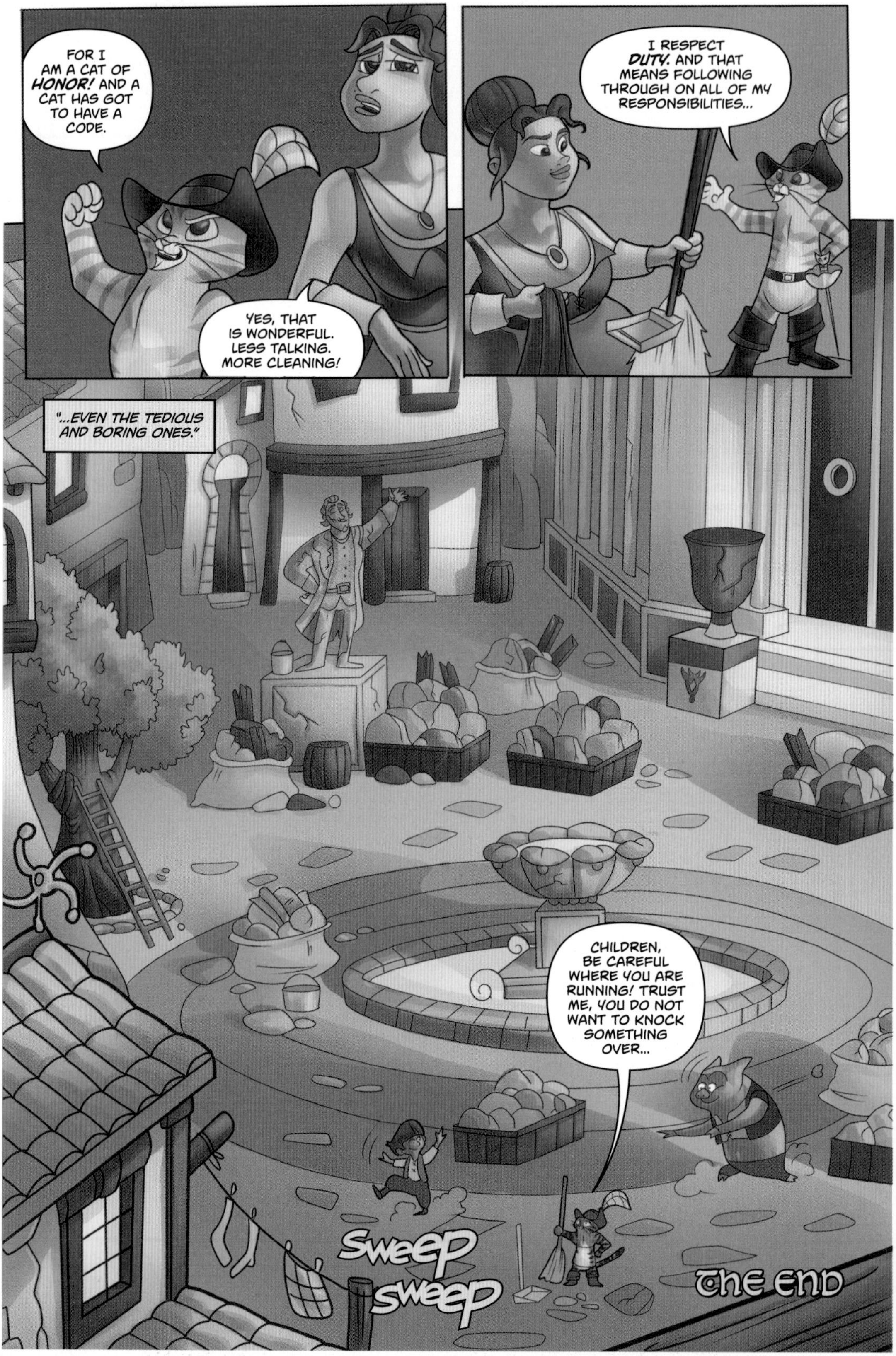
FOR I AM A CAT OF HONOR! AND A CAT HAS GOT TO HAVE A CODE.
YES, THAT IS WONDERFUL. LESS TALKING. MORE CLEANING!
I RESPECT DUTY. AND THAT MEANS FOLLOWING THROUGH ON ALL OF MY RESPONSIBILITIES...
"...EVEN THE TEDIOUS AND BORING ONES."
CHILDREN, BE CAREFUL WHERE YOU ARE RUNNING! TRUST ME, YOU DO NOT WANT TO KNOCK SOMETHING OVER...
SWEEP SWEEP
THE END

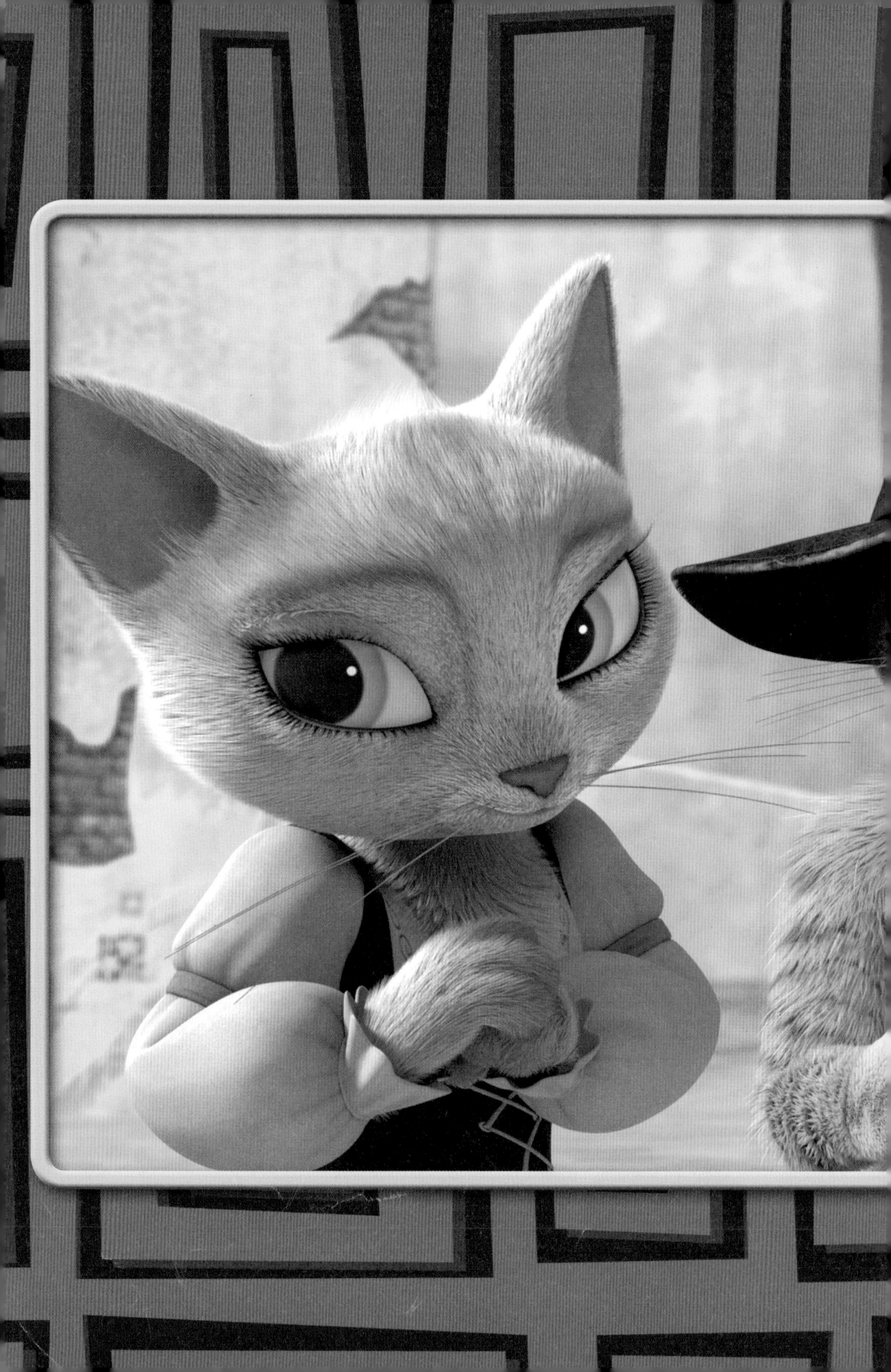

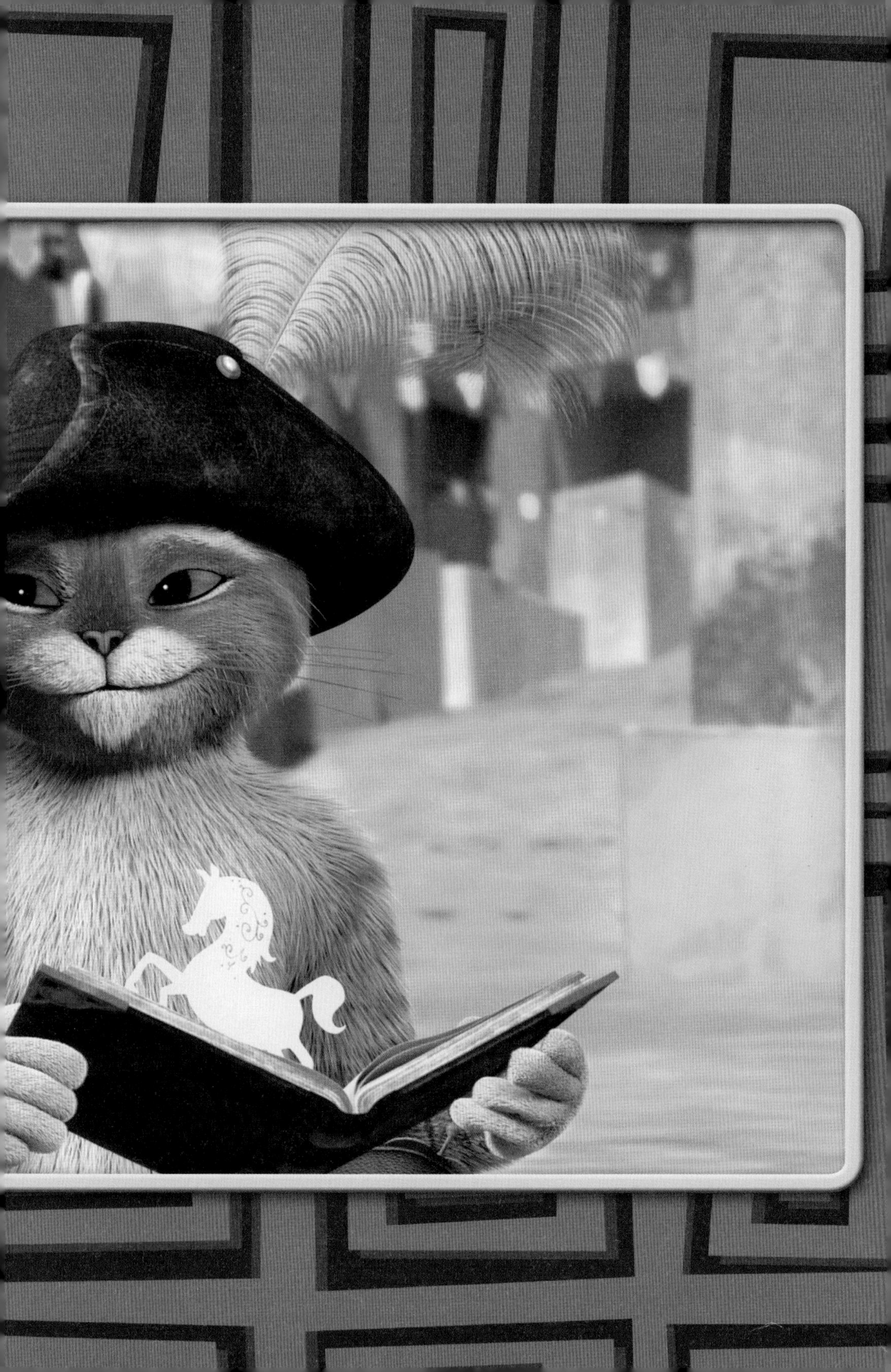

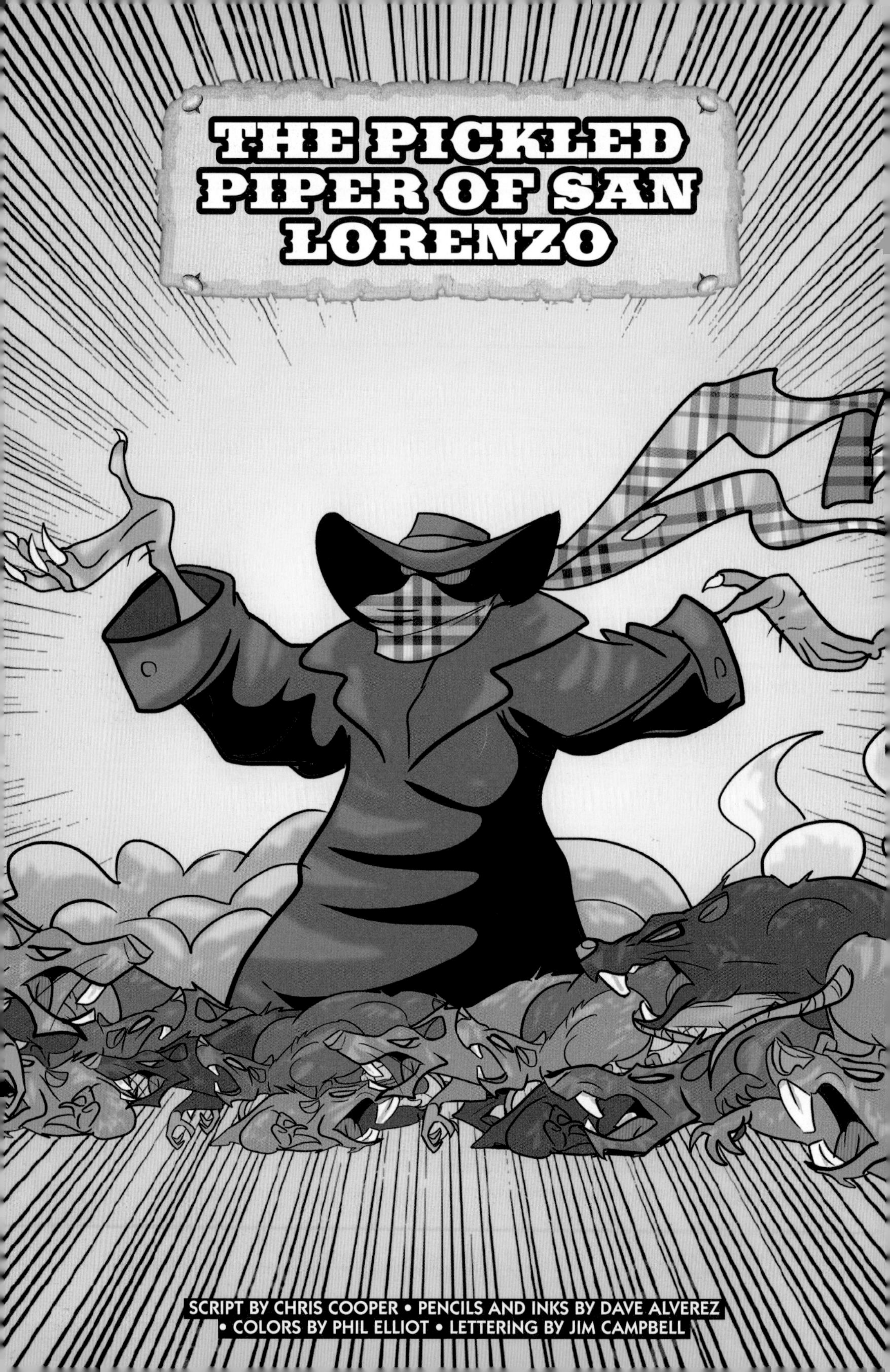
THE PICKLED PIPER OF SAN LORENZO
SCRIPT BY CHRIS COOPER • PENCILS AND INKS BY DAVE ALVEREZ
• COLORS BY PHIL ELLIOT • LETTERING BY JIM CAMPBELL

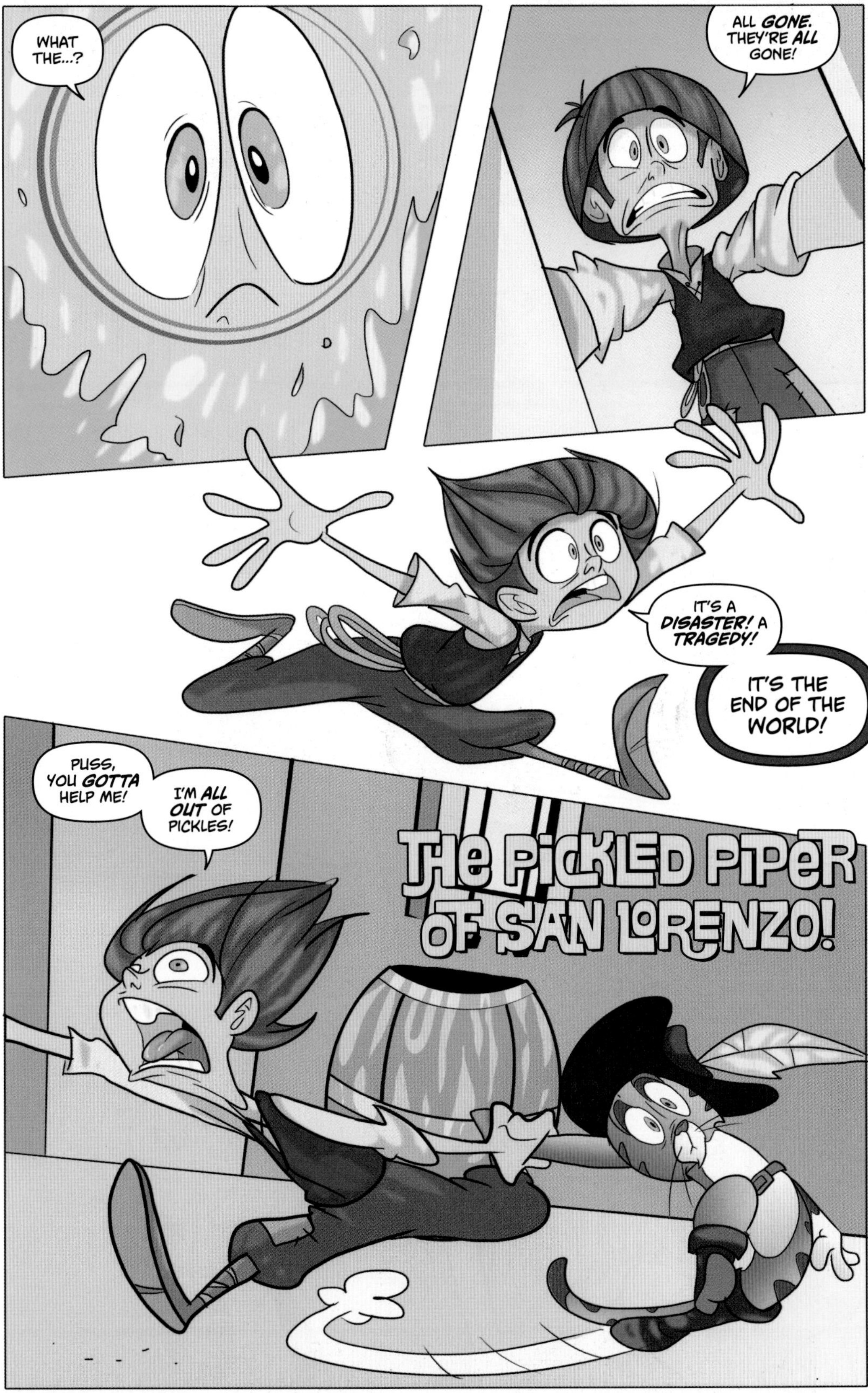
WHAT THE...?
ALL GONE. THEY'RE ALL GONE!
IT'S A DISASTER! A TRAGEDY!
IT'S THE END OF THE WORLD!
PUSS, YOU GOTTA HELP ME!
I'M ALL OUT OF PICKLES!
THE PICKLED PIPER OF SAN LORENZO!

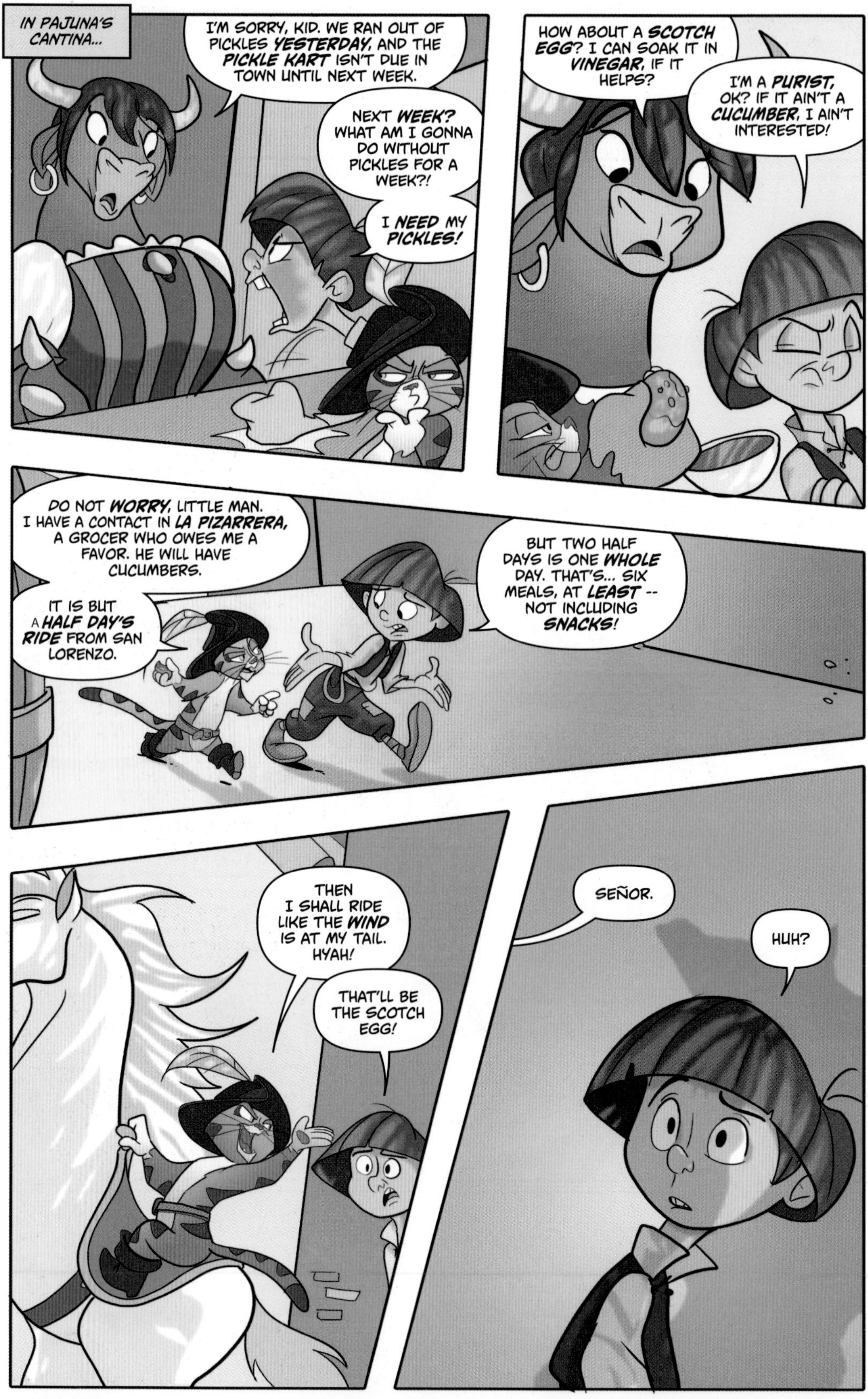
IN PAJUNA'S CANTINA...
I'M SORRY, KID. WE RAN OUT OF PICKLES YESTERDAY, AND THE PICKLE KART ISN'T DUE IN TOWN UNTIL NEXT WEEK.
NEXT WEEK? WHAT AM I GONNA DO WITHOUT PICKLES FOR A WEEK?!
I NEED MY PICKLES!
HOW ABOUT A SCOTCH EGG? I CAN SOAK IT IN VINEGAR, IF IT HELPS?
I'M A PURIST, OK? IF IT AIN'T A CUCUMBER, I AIN'T INTERESTED!
DO NOT WORRY, LITTLE MAN. I HAVE A CONTACT IN LA PIZARRERA, A GROCER WHO OWES ME A FAVOR. HE WILL HAVE CUCUMBERS.
IT IS BUT A HALF DAY'S RIDE FROM SAN LORENZO.
BUT TWO HALF DAYS IS ONE WHOLE DAY. THAT'S... SIX MEALS, AT LEAST -- NOT INCLUDING SNACKS!
THEN I SHALL RIDE LIKE THE WIND IS AT MY TAIL. HYAH!
THAT'LL BE THE SCOTCH EGG!
SEÑOR.
HUH?

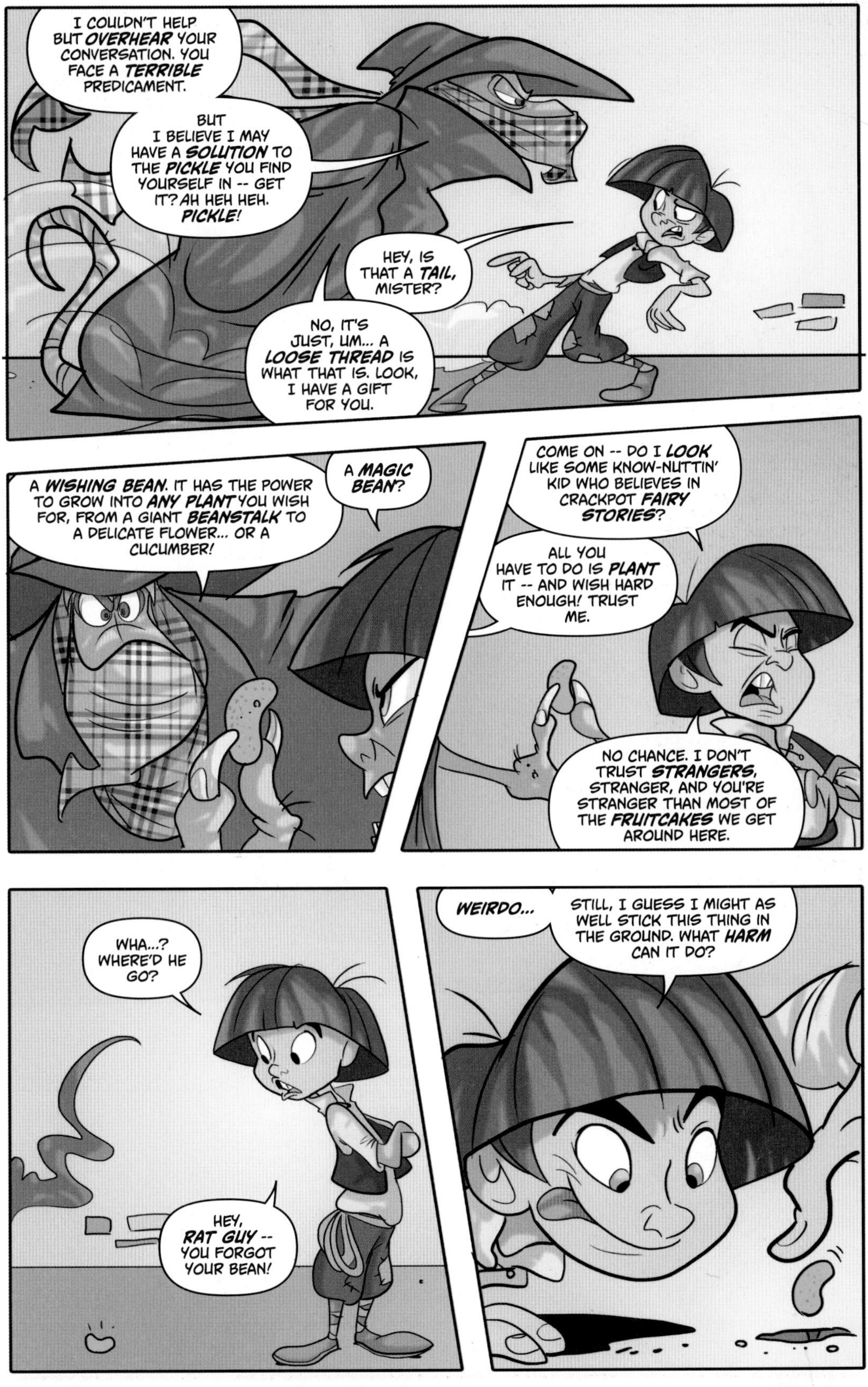

I COULDN'T HELP BUT OVERHEAR YOUR CONVERSATION. YOU FACE A TERRIBLE PREDICAMENT.
BUT I BELIEVE I MAY HAVE A SOLUTION TO THE PICKLE YOU FIND YOURSELF IN -- GET IT? AH HEH HEH. PICKLE!
HEY, IS THAT A TAIL, MISTER?
NO, IT'S JUST, UM... A LOOSE THREAD IS WHAT THAT IS. LOOK, I HAVE A GIFT FOR YOU.
A WISHING BEAN. IT HAS THE POWER TO GROW INTO ANY PLANT YOU WISH FOR, FROM A GIANT BEANSTALK TO A DELICATE FLOWER... OR A CUCUMBER!
A MAGIC BEAN?
COME ON -- DO I LOOK LIKE SOME KNOW-NUTTIN' KID WHO BELIEVES IN CRACKPOT FAIRY STORIES?
ALL YOU HAVE TO DO IS PLANT IT -- AND WISH HARD ENOUGH! TRUST ME.
NO CHANCE. I DON'T TRUST STRANGERS, STRANGER, AND YOU'RE STRANGER THAN MOST OF THE FRUITCAKES WE GET AROUND HERE.
WHA...? WHERE'D HE GO?
HEY, RAT GUY -- YOU FORGOT YOUR BEAN!
WEIRDO...
STILL, I GUESS I MIGHT AS WELL STICK THIS THING IN THE GROUND. WHAT HARM CAN IT DO?

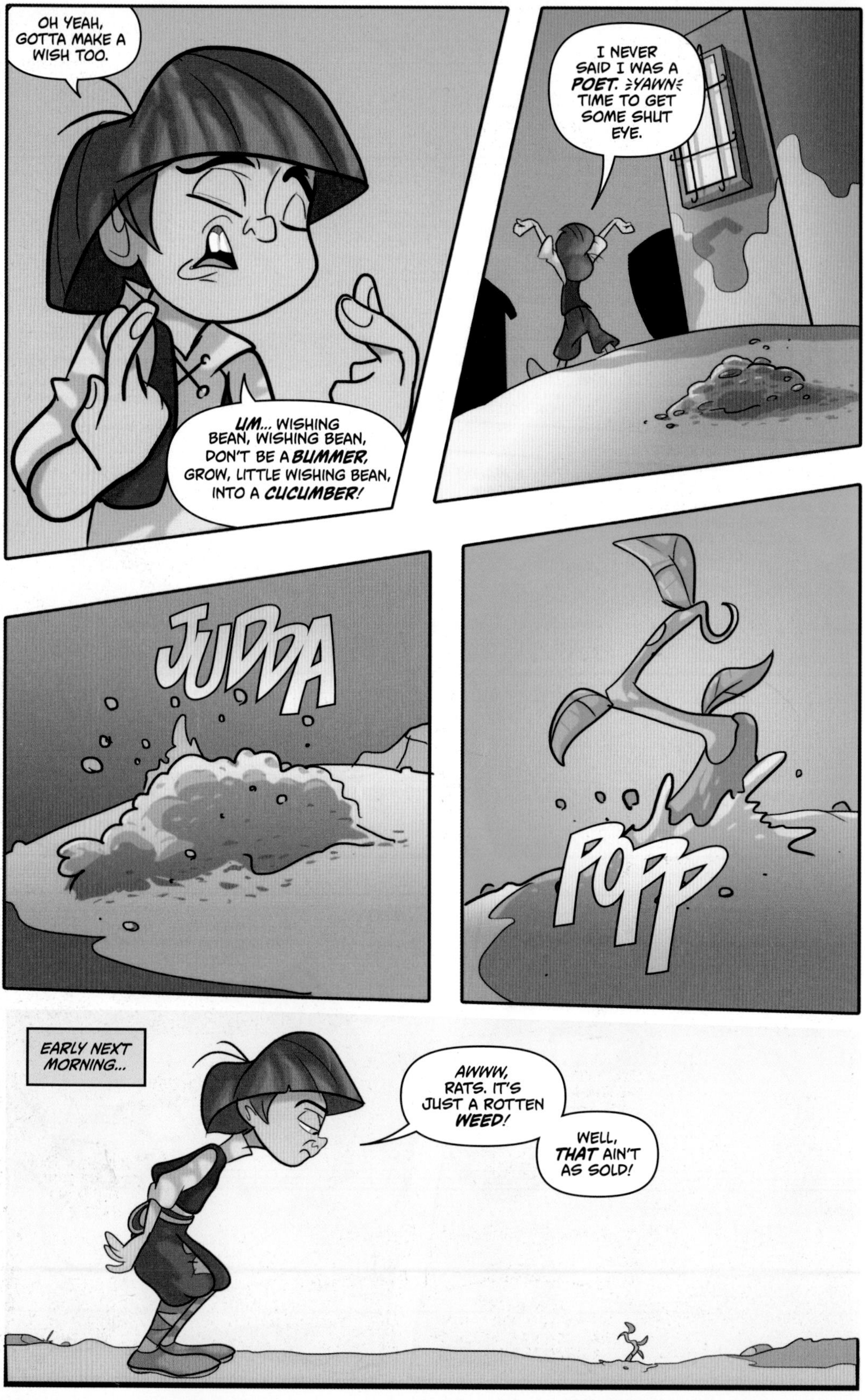
OH YEAH, GOTTA MAKE A WISH TOO.
UM... WISHING BEAN, WISHING BEAN, DON'T BE A BUMMER, GROW, LITTLE WISHING BEAN, INTO A CUCUMBER!
I NEVER SAID I WAS A POET. YAWN TIME TO GET SOME SHUT EYE.
JUDDA
POPP
EARLY NEXT MORNING...
AWWW, RATS. IT'S JUST A ROTTEN WEED!
WELL, THAT AIN'T AS SOLD!

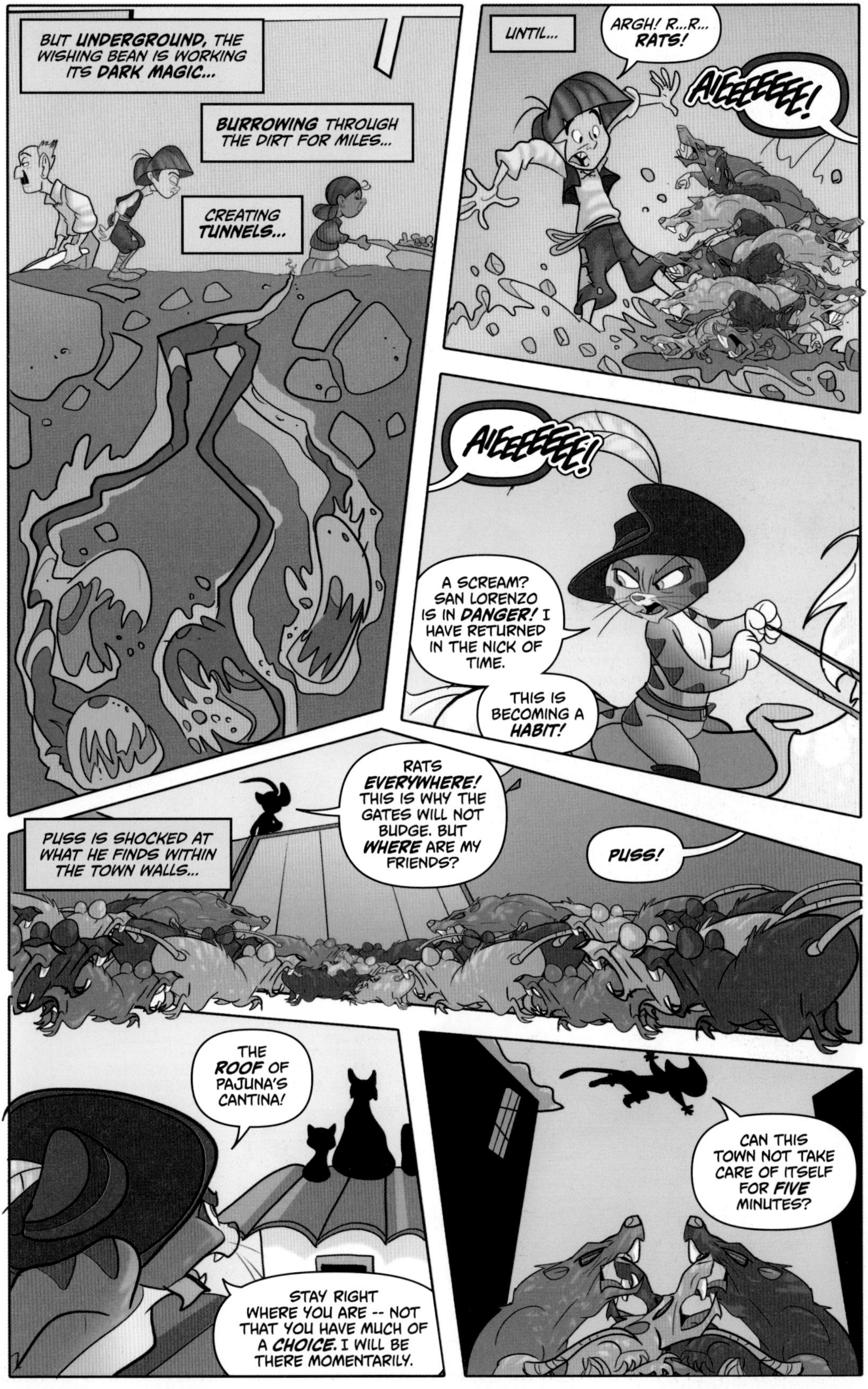
BUT UNDERGROUND, THE WISHING BEAN IS WORKING ITS DARK MAGIC...
BURROWING THROUGH THE DIRT FOR MILES...
CREATING TUNNELS...
UNTIL...
ARGH! R...R... RATS!
AIEEEEEEE!
AIEEEEEEE!
A SCREAM? SAN LORENZO IS IN DANGER! I HAVE RETURNED IN THE NICK OF TIME.
THIS IS BECOMING A HABIT!
PUSS IS SHOCKED AT WHAT HE FINDS WITHIN THE TOWN WALLS...
RATS EVERYWHERE! THIS IS WHY THE GATES WILL NOT BUDGE. BUT WHERE ARE MY FRIENDS?
PUSS!
THE ROOF OF PAJUNA'S CANTINA!
STAY RIGHT WHERE YOU ARE -- NOT THAT YOU HAVE MUCH OF A CHOICE. I WILL BE THERE MOMENTARILY.
CAN THIS TOWN NOT TAKE CARE OF ITSELF FOR FIVE MINUTES?

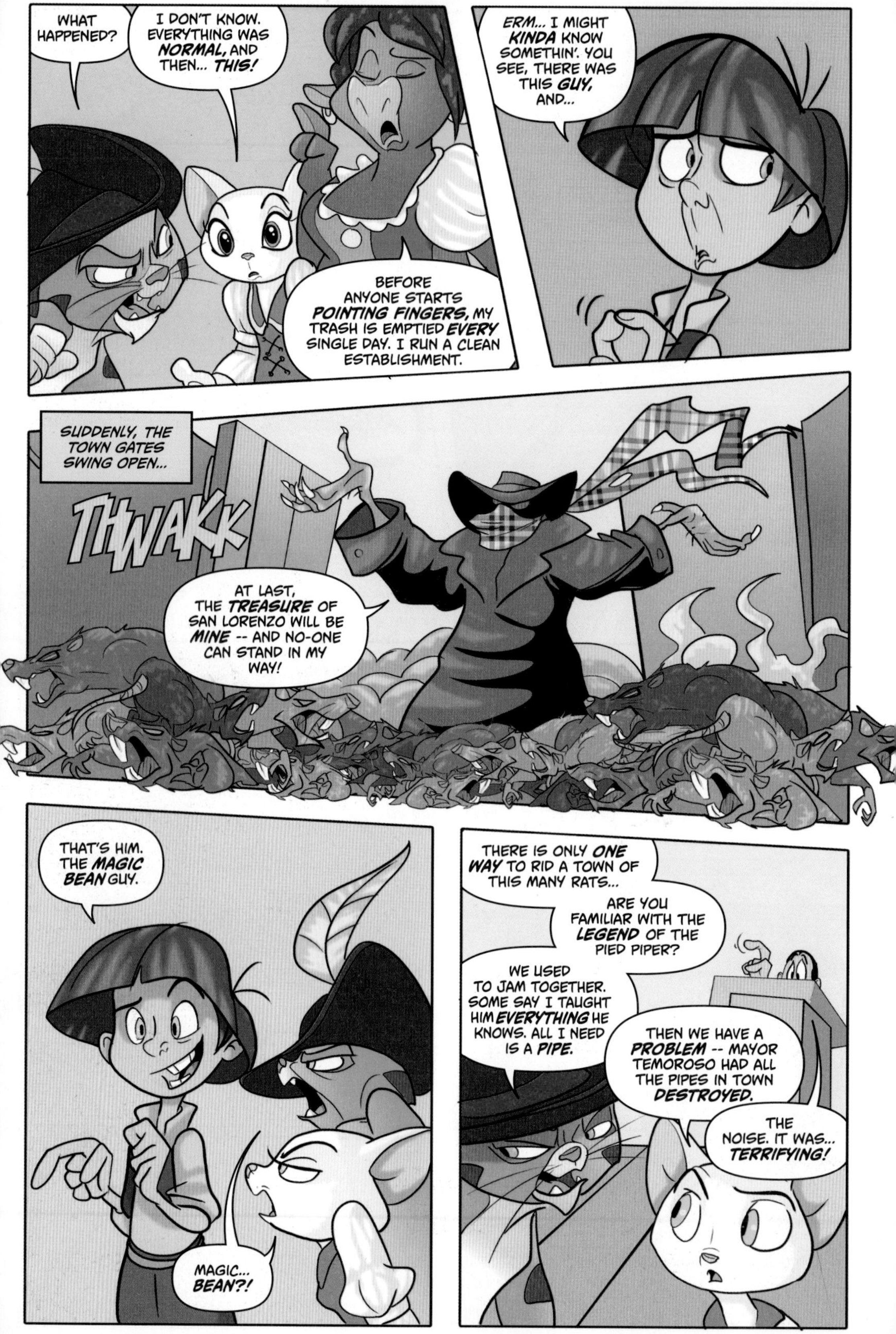

WHAT HAPPENED?
I DON'T KNOW. EVERYTHING WAS NORMAL, AND THEN... THIS!
BEFORE ANYONE STARTS POINTING FINGERS, MY TRASH IS EMPTIED EVERY SINGLE DAY. I RUN A CLEAN ESTABLISHMENT.
ERM... I MIGHT KINDA KNOW SOMETHIN'. YOU SEE, THERE WAS THIS GUY, AND...
SUDDENLY, THE TOWN GATES SWING OPEN...
THWAKK
AT LAST, THE TREASURE OF SAN LORENZO WILL BE MINE -- AND NO-ONE CAN STAND IN MY WAY!
THAT'S HIM. THE MAGIC BEAN GUY.
MAGIC... BEAN?!
THERE IS ONLY ONE WAY TO RID A TOWN OF THIS MANY RATS...
ARE YOU FAMILIAR WITH THE LEGEND OF THE PIED PIPER?
WE USED TO JAM TOGETHER. SOME SAY I TAUGHT HIM EVERYTHING HE KNOWS. ALL I NEED IS A PIPE.
THEN WE HAVE A PROBLEM -- MAYOR TEMOROSO HAD ALL THE PIPES IN TOWN DESTROYED.
THE NOISE. IT WAS... TERRIFYING!

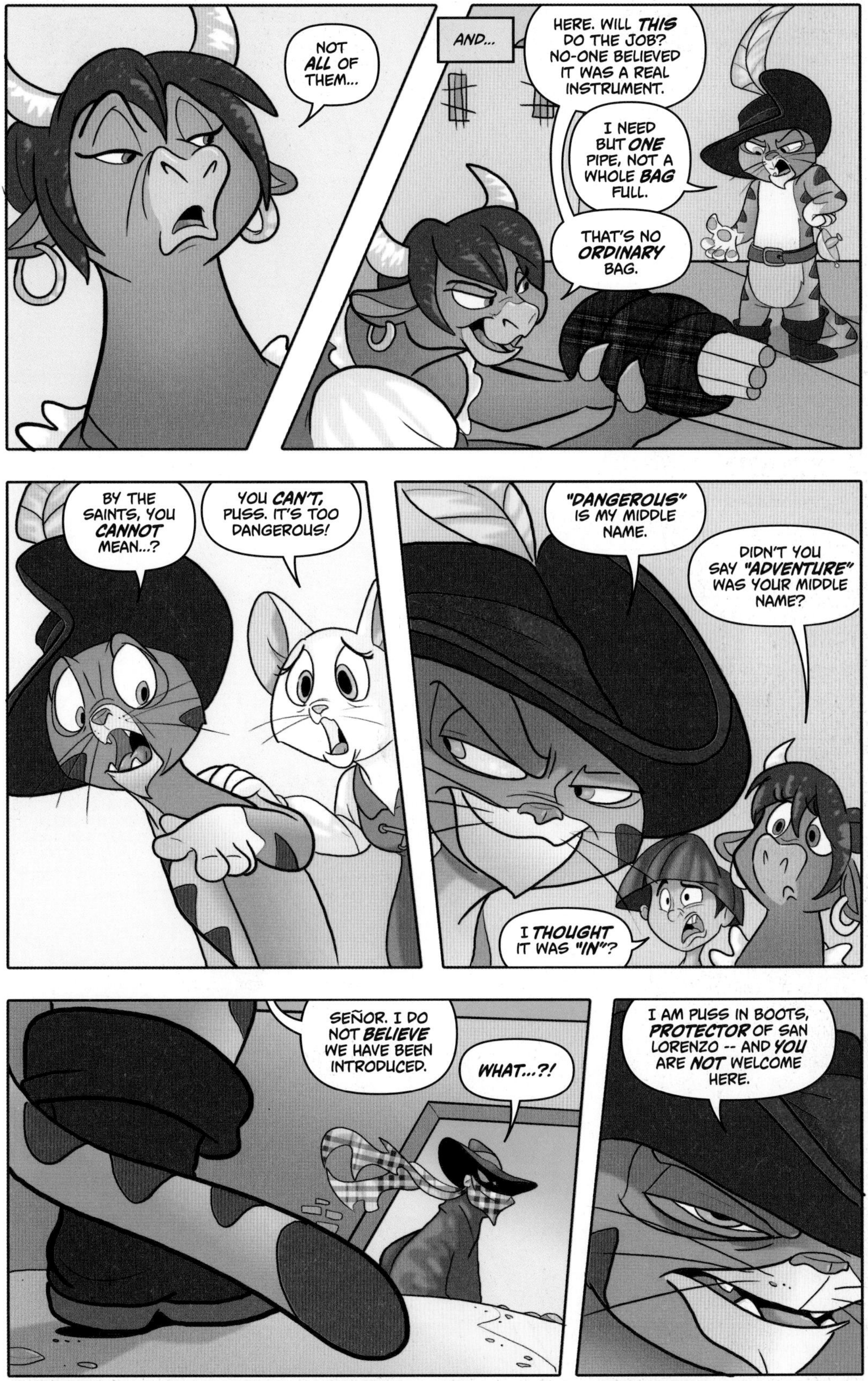

NOT ALL OF THEM...
AND...
HERE. WILL THIS DO THE JOB? NO-ONE BELIEVED IT WAS A REAL INSTRUMENT.
I NEED BUT ONE PIPE, NOT A WHOLE BAG FULL.
THAT'S NO ORDINARY BAG.
BY THE SAINTS, YOU CANNOT MEAN...?
YOU CAN'T, PUSS. IT'S TOO DANGEROUS!
"DANGEROUS" IS MY MIDDLE NAME.
DIDN'T YOU SAY "ADVENTURE" WAS YOUR MIDDLE NAME?
I THOUGHT IT WAS "IN"?
SEÑOR. I DO NOT BELIEVE WE HAVE BEEN INTRODUCED.
WHAT...?!
I AM PUSS IN BOOTS, PROTECTOR OF SAN LORENZO -- AND YOU ARE NOT WELCOME HERE.

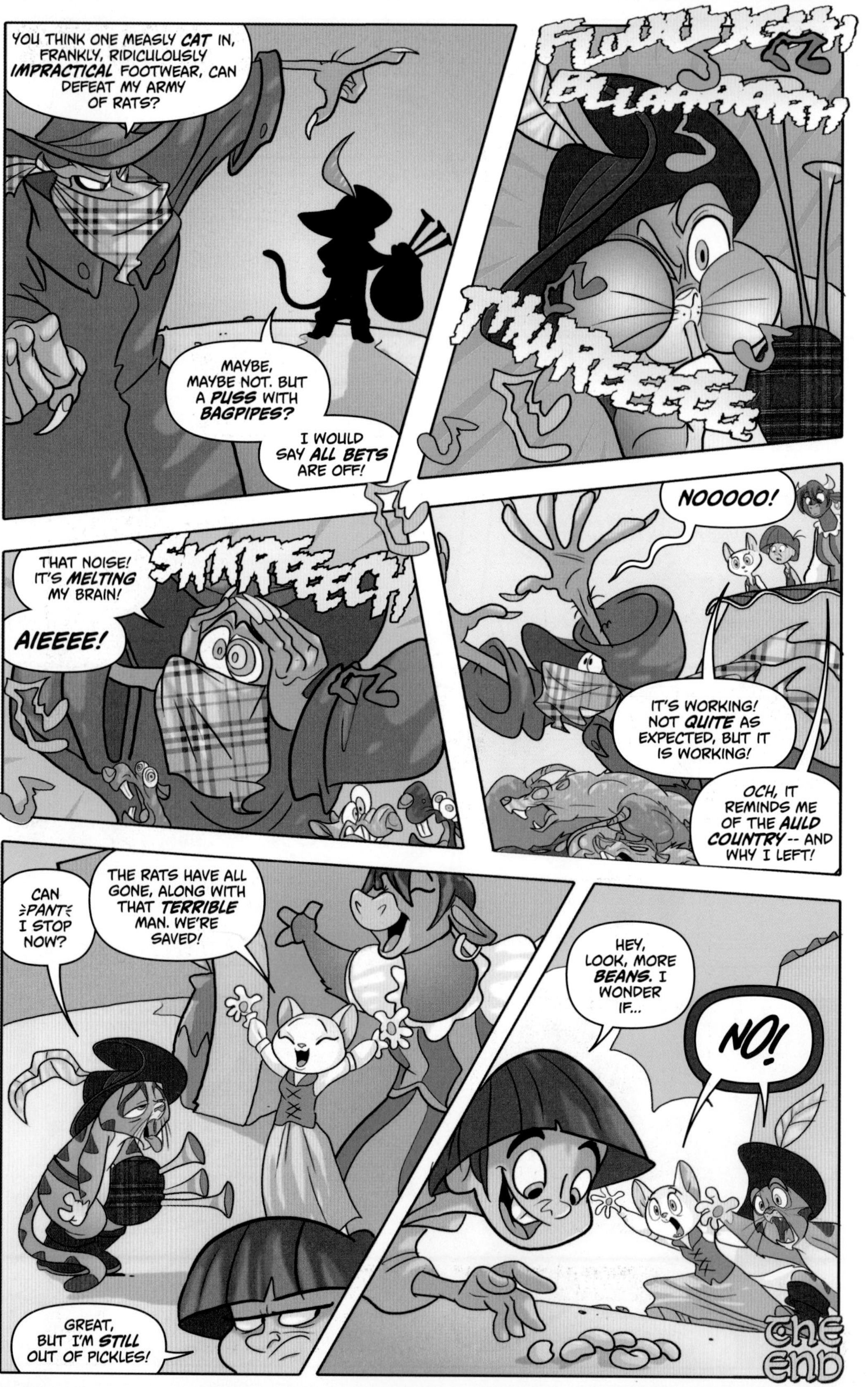

YOU THINK ONE MEASLY CAT IN, FRANKLY, RIDICULOUSLY IMPRACTICAL FOOTWEAR, CAN DEFEAT MY ARMY OF RATS?
MAYBE, MAYBE NOT. BUT A PUSS WITH BAGPIPES?
I WOULD SAY ALL BETS ARE OFF!
FLOOUGH
BLLAAAARH
THWREEEEE
THAT NOISE! IT'S MELTING MY BRAIN!
AIEEEE!
SKKREEECH
NOOOOO!
IT'S WORKING! NOT QUITE AS EXPECTED, BUT IT IS WORKING!
OCH, IT REMINDS ME OF THE AULD COUNTRY -- AND WHY I LEFT!
CAN ≷PANT≶ I STOP NOW?
THE RATS HAVE ALL GONE, ALONG WITH THAT TERRIBLE MAN. WE'RE SAVED!
GREAT, BUT I'M STILL OUT OF PICKLES!
HEY, LOOK, MORE BEANS. I WONDER IF...
NO!
THE END

TITAN COMICS GRAPHIC NOVELS

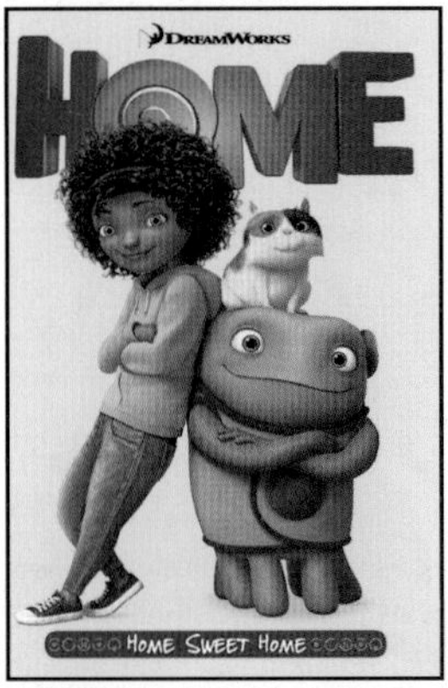
DreamWorks
HOME
HOME SWEET HOME

DREAMWORKS HOME: HOME SWEET HOME

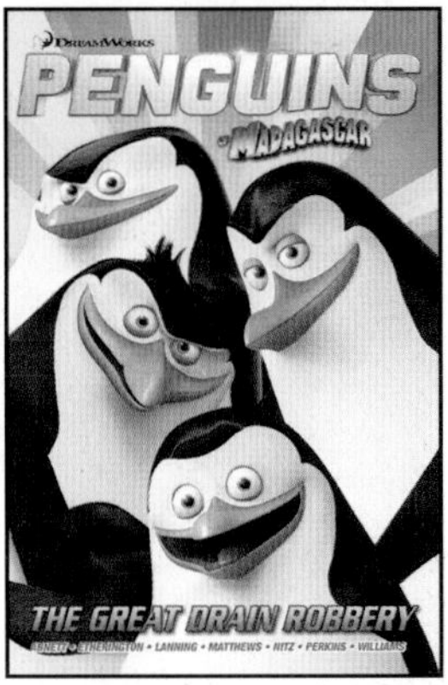
DreamWorks
PENGUINS
of MADAGASCAR
THE GREAT DRAIN ROBBERY

PENGUINS OF MADAGASCAR:
THE GREAT DRAIN ROBBERY

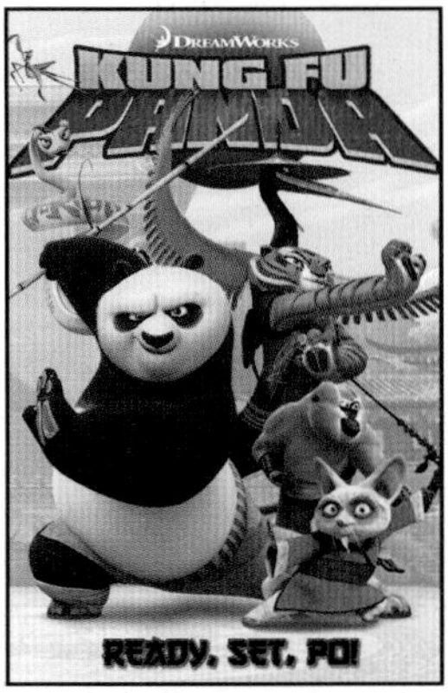
DreamWorks
KUNG FU PANDA
READY, SET, PO!

KUNG FU PANDA:
READY, SET, PO!

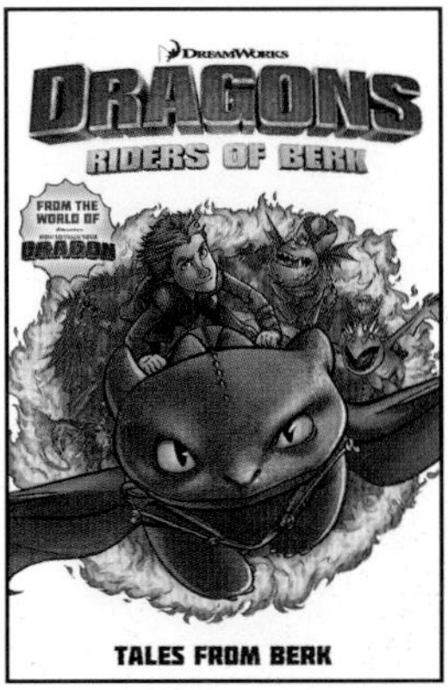
DreamWorks
DRAGONS
RIDERS OF BERK
FROM THE WORLD OF
DRAGON
TALES FROM BERK

DREAMWORKS DRAGONS:
RIDERS OF BERK – TALES FROM BERK

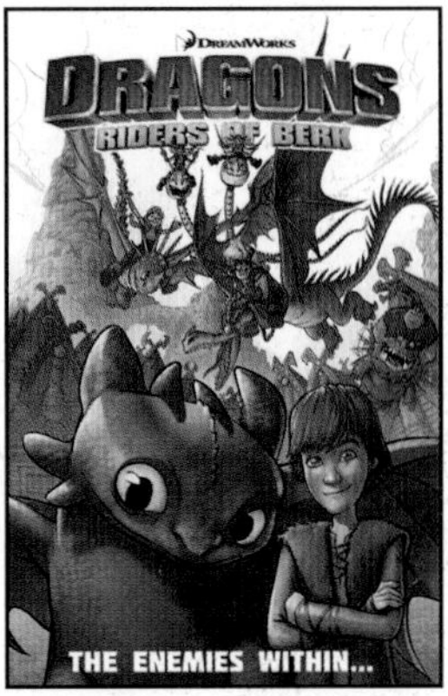
DreamWorks
DRAGONS
RIDERS OF BERK
THE ENEMIES WITHIN...

DREAMWORKS DRAGONS:
RIDERS OF BERK – THE ENEMIES WITHIN

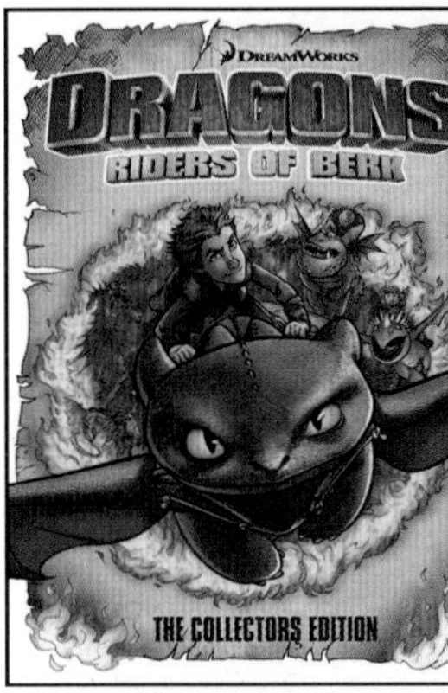
DreamWorks
DRAGONS
RIDERS OF BERK
THE COLLECTORS EDITION

DREAMWORKS DRAGONS: RIDERS OF BERK
COLLECTORS EDITION

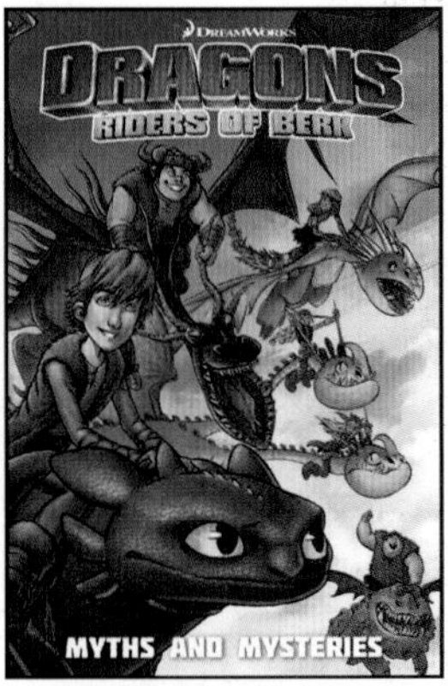
DreamWorks
DRAGONS
RIDERS OF BERK
MYTHS AND MYSTERIES

DREAMWORKS DRAGONS:
MYTHS AND MYSTERIES
COMING SOON

WWW.TITAN-COMICS.COM

TITAN COMICS

DREAMWORKS ANIMATION SKG

TITAN COMICS COMIC BOOKS